PENGUIN BOOKS

GANGLANDS BRAZIL

Born in Essex in 1964, Ross Kemp is best known for his portrayal of Grant Mitchell in *EastEnders*. His father was a senior detective with the Metropolitan Police force and as a result crime has always fascinated Kemp. In 2007 *Ross Kemp on Gangs* won a BAFTA for Best Factual Series.

D1434108

ROSS KEMP

GANG LANDS
BRAZIL

PENGUIN BOOKS

PENGUIN BOOKS

Published by the Penguin Group
Penguin Books Ltd, 80 Strand, London WC2R ORL, England
Penguin Group (USA) Inc., 375 Hudson Street, New York, New York 10014, USA
Penguin Group (Canada), 90 Eglinton Avenue East, Suite 700, Toronto, Ontario, Canada M4P 2Y3
(a division of Pearson Penguin Canada Inc.)
Penguin Ireland, 25 St Stephen's Green, Dublin 2, Ireland (a division of Penguin Books Ltd)
Penguin Group (Australia), 250 Camberwell Road, Camberwell, Victoria 3124, Australia
(a division of Pearson Australia Group Pty Ltd)
Penguin Books India Pvt Ltd, 11 Community Centre, Panchsheel Park, New Delhi – 110 017, India
Penguin Group (NZ), 67 Apollo Drive, Rosedale, North Shore 0632, New Zealand
(a division of Pearson New Zealand Ltd)
Penguin Books (South Africa) (Pty) Ltd, 24 Sturdee Avenue, Rosebank, Johannesburg 2196, South Africa

Penguin Books Ltd, Registered Offices: 80 Strand, London WC2R ORL, England

penguin.com

First published 2009
1

Text copyright © Ross Kemp, 2009
Map copyright © Tom Sanderson, 2009
All rights reserved

The moral right of the author and illustrator has been asserted

Set in Garamond MT 12.5/15.25pt
Typeset by Palimpsest Book Production Limited, Grangemouth, Stirlingshire
Made and printed in England by Clays Ltd, St Ives plc

British Library Cataloguing in Publication Data
A CIP catalogue record for this book is available from the British Library

ISBN: 978–0–141–32589–7

www.greenpenguin.co.uk

Penguin Books is committed to a sustainable future
for our business, our readers and our planet.
The book in your hands is made from paper
certified by the Forest Stewardship Council.

World Map

BRAZIL

.Rio De Janeiro

1. Dead Baby

A storm was coming.

Dark clouds rolled in towards Rio de Janeiro, looming above the luxury high-rise apartments and the hillside shanty towns alike. The atmosphere was taut with the threat of rain. On top of Corcovado mountain, the giant statue of Jesus that looked over the city had its arms outstretched, as though helpless in the face of the oncoming storm. Down on the beaches of Copacabana and Ipanema, glamorous bathers glanced up at the darkening sky and began pulling on T-shirts over their bikinis and swimming trunks. Raucous games of beach football came to a ragged end as players ran for shelter.

As the first spots of rain began to fall, Vitor 'Nene' Barbosa boarded a bus down by the beachfront, a basketball nestling under his arm. He was dressed in a tracksuit and his cropped black hair was still damp from his post-training shower. As he moved along the aisle towards the back of the bus, the driver called out a cheery greeting. Even though Nene had only just turned sixteen, everybody in Rio knew him – a basketball prodigy, he was destined for great things.

His nickname meant Baby – a joke, seeing as how Nene had towered over his friends since he was a child. Now more than two metres tall, he was still growing. Nene played centre for Flamengo Petrobras, Rio's basketball team. The pivotal position on court, centres operated in and around the basket, where the rough-and-tumble demanded a muscular, athletic presence. You didn't normally play there at sixteen. But then normal rules didn't apply to Nene.

It wasn't only his height that made him special. The first time Nene had walked out on to the basketball court, his trainers squeaking on the hardwood surface, it felt as though he had come home. Things just made sense to him there. While his opponents tried to barge and muscle their way to the basket, Nene glided, snatching rebounds and sinking fade-aways as though the opposition wasn't even there. From the tip-off to the final buzzer, to him games felt like long, beautiful dreams.

Thirty points against Flamengo's rivals Brasilia in the last game – when Nene had been almost unplayable – had increased the hype surrounding him to fever pitch. Now there was talk of a call-up to the national team, even rumours that American scouts from the NBA were going to travel all the way down to Brazil to watch him. Nene had spent years gazing at the basketball posters that plastered his bedroom walls, dreaming of becoming the next Kobe Bryant. The thought that he might one day play on the same court as him made Nene dizzy with excitement.

It was about more than sporting glory, though. Every-one knew that there was serious money to be made in

America, million-dollar contracts up for grabs. To Nene, who lived with his mother and two brothers in a small house in Rocinha – the largest *favela*, or shanty town, in Rio – such riches seemed unimaginable. Money was tight at the best of times, but recently Nene's mother had been laid up ill in bed, and the money Nene received for playing basketball and working in a supermarket was barely putting food on the table. If he could only impress an NBA scout, Nene told himself, then none of his family would have to worry about money ever again.

The bus driver honked his horn angrily, interrupting Nene's train of thought. There was a squeal of brakes and the bus came to an abrupt halt.

It was raining heavily now, large drops drumming against the windows. Peering outside, Nene saw that they had stopped at a quiet intersection on the edge of the Zona Sul, Rio's affluent tourist district. A group of teenagers had fanned out across the middle of the road, blocking the bus's path. They were dressed identically, in all-black T-shirts and knee-length shorts. His heart sinking, Nene saw that they were carrying guns: a deadly combination of pistols and semi-automatic rifles. The bus was being hijacked.

Perhaps he should have been more surprised – but then, gangs were a part of Rio's life as much as the beaches and the *Carnaval*. Made up predominantly of teenage boys, they maintained their own distinct identities and colours, marking out their territories in the *favelas* with lurid graffiti. Most of the time the gangs stayed on their own turf, concentrating on drug dealing and warring with their rivals. On the rare occasions that they ventured out en masse into downtown Rio, chaos ensued: robberies, rioting, even shoot-outs with the police.

Growing up in Rocinha, Nene knew all about infamous Rio gangs such as the Compadres and Quarto Comando. But the Compadres' colours were red and Quarto Comando's green; they wouldn't dress in all black like these guys. He forced himself to stay calm. Sports stars were cherished in Rio – even among the *favela* gangs. They weren't about to shoot holes into a *carioca*, a local boy, who had made good. He just had to keep quiet and do as he was told.

A dark-skinned boy in orange-tinted Ray-Bans stepped to the head of the gang and gestured at the bus driver to open the door. Then they strutted aboard the bus, their confidence bolstered by the firearms at their sides.

'We're the Comando Negro,' the boy with the sunglasses called out confidently. 'Get your money out now. Any trouble and we'll start firing.'

Immediately the passengers began rooting through their pockets and handbags, removing watches and jewellery in their eagerness to cooperate. Nene pulled out his wallet, careful not to make any sudden movements. He had never heard of the Comando Negro before and new gangs always spelled trouble – with everything to prove, and reputations to build, they tended to have twitchy trigger fingers.

The gang moved down the aisle, shouting at the passengers to throw their valuables into sports bags. One boy remained at the door of the bus, scanning the road for signs of the police. Whoever these guys were, Nene thought to himself, they looked pretty professional for a new outfit.

A black teenager with bleached-blond hair and a deep facial scar stopped by Nene's seat, his wide pupils and trembling hands bearing the hallmarks of heavy cocaine use. As the boy pointed at his open sports bag with a snub-nosed pistol, Nene tossed in his wallet, aware that he was throwing his family's dinner away with it.

Once the passengers had been stripped of their money, the gang filed quickly back off the bus. It had been a lightning raid. The blond-haired boy made to follow them, then turned back to Nene.

'I know you,' he said. 'Basketball player, aren't you?'

Nene nodded.

'We played against your team a couple of years back.'

'Yeah?'

'Yeah.' The boy nodded. 'You scored a lot of points that day. Didn't make me look so good.'

Nene shrugged. 'Didn't mean anything by it. All in the game, you know?'

The blond boy replied by cocking the hammer of his pistol and pressing it into the side of Nene's head. The metal barrel felt icy cold on his skin.

'You don't look so big now,' said the boy.

'I don't want any trouble,' Nene replied softly, his pulse racing. 'You've had my wallet. I haven't got anything else.'

The boy dug the barrel deeper into Nene's skin, forcing his head back against the window. He smiled coldly.

A whistle came from the front of the bus.

'Stripe!' the boy with the orange Ray-Bans called out. 'Angel said no pissing about, remember? If you've got his wallet, let's get the hell out of here.'

Stripe shot an angry glare at the other boy and then pulled the gun away from Nene's head.

'Next time,' he said.

As the boy walked away, Nene's shoulders slumped with relief. Looking down at his hands, he saw that they were shaking uncontrollably.

As the Comando Negro hurried off the bus and towards their 50cc motorbikes on the corner of the intersection, the sound of sirens struck up an insistent wail in the background. Joker – the boy with the orange Ray-Bans – smiled. It was going like clockwork, just as Angel had said it would. The passengers had handed over their valuables without a murmur. These beachfront people were all the same: soft.

He was about to speed away on his motorbike when he saw that Stripe had stopped in his tracks, a thoughtful look on his face.

'Come on, Stripe! We're done!'

The blond-haired boy ignored him. Turning abruptly on his heel, he walked back through the rain towards the bus.

'Where the hell are you going now?' Joker called out. 'The police'll be here soon!'

Deep in his heart, however, he knew exactly where

Stripe was going – Joker had known him long enough for that. Perhaps Angel could have stopped him, but then Angel wasn't here. All Joker could do was watch, revving his bike engine in frustration. Through the bus windows he saw Stripe reboard the vehicle and stride back along the aisle towards the tall boy with the basketball. Stripe said something, raising his gun.

There was a loud popping sound and then a spray of red liquid splattered against the window where the basket-baller's head had been a moment beforehand.

As a chorus of horrified screams went up from the bus's passengers, Stripe walked nonchalantly back down the steps and towards Joker.

'What?' he said, catching Joker's sideways glance. 'He made me look bad.'

Kicking his motorbike into life, Stripe drove quickly away down a side street. Joker swore loudly and gestured for the rest of the Comando Negro to follow suit. They sped off in an angry whine of engines, leaving the bus stationary in the middle of the road, the rain beginning to collect in puddles around it.

2. Blood Relative

The children filed out of Sacred Heart School amid riotous laughter, relieved to have escaped for another day. To Luiz Alves, who was walking quickly through the jostling crowds, the loud shouts and giggles sounded like a chorus of zoo animals. Fifteen years old, with light-brown skin, curly black hair and broad shoulders that filled out his white school shirt, Luiz moved with a quiet self-assurance that suggested he didn't mind being on his own.

Sacred Heart was a private school set in the heart of Botafogo, a bustling, middle-class neighbourhood of Rio, where the streets were dotted with cafes, museums and bookshops. With the school charging expensive fees, the pupils were a mixture of foreign students and children from well-to-do local families. English was the language heard in the corridors and the classrooms, not Brazilian Portuguese. While Sacred Heart could boast state-of-the-art computer rooms and sports facilities, the security cameras at the school exits and the high iron railings provided a constant reminder that not everywhere in Rio was as affluent, or as safe.

As Luiz walked away down the street, a football flew

past his ear and he heard a familiar voice cry out, 'Hey, asshole!'

He turned to see his friend Gui standing by the gates, his arm draped over the shoulder of a pretty blonde girl. 'We're going down to the beach,' he called out. 'You coming?'

Luiz shook his head. 'It's Ana's birthday,' he shouted back. 'I've got to go home.'

Gui shrugged. 'Your loss, asshole! See you tomorrow.'

With a wave, Luiz turned away. As he walked off, he heard Gui's girl scream with laughter. Ordinarily Luiz wouldn't have thought twice about going with them, but today was different. His younger sister, Ana, was turning fourteen and he wanted to be home when she got back from school. Their foster parents, Francesco and Mariella, were in São Paulo for two weeks, researching an exclusive story for *O Globo*, the newspaper they both worked for. When they returned, the family was going out for a special meal in one of the posh restaurants in the Zona Sul, but for tonight it was going to be just Luiz and Ana.

Life hadn't always been so comfortable. Luiz and Ana had grown up in very different surroundings, in the sprawling *favela* of Santa Marta that clung to the hillside overlooking Botafogo. Abandoned by their dad after Ana's birth, they were brought up by their mum on her own. When she succumbed to cancer, a local priest had come to the rescue, taking Luiz and Ana in and contacting an adoption agency. A week later, Francesco and Mariella had arrived to collect them from the mission, and had then introduced them to their new home in Botafogo.

Settling in hadn't been easy. On Luiz's first day at Sacred Heart, one of the kids had made the mistake of laughing at his coarse *favela* accent. It had taken three teachers to prise Luiz off him and the other boy had had to go to hospital. Luiz had nearly been expelled on his very first day; after that, the other pupils gave him a wide, wary berth, as if he were a dangerous animal or a leper. In the end it had been Gui – irrepressible, fun-loving Gui – who had plonked himself down next to Luiz during a maths lesson and started cracking jokes. They had been best friends ever since.

Gradually Luiz had begun to feel more at home. He managed to rein in his temper and stopped taking offence at every perceived slight. It had been two years since he had last been in a fight – Ana joked that he was turning into a pacifist. Luiz knew that his anger would never entirely disappear, though, that it bubbled somewhere deep within his soul. Nor had he forgotten about Santa Marta. For all the dangers of the *favela*, Luiz missed its vibrancy, the energy that crackled through the streets. He wasn't stupid – he knew what his life would be like if he was still up there. He'd probably be in one of the gangs, selling drugs. There were only so many ways you could make money in the *favelas*, especially without parents, and you had to eat. Even so, walking underneath the shadow of Santa Marta every day, it was hard not to feel the occasional pang of regret.

Shielding his eyes from the sun, Luiz looked up the hillside at the cramped dwellings piled on top of one another, at the makeshift buildings with their slanting roofs and the winding, treacherously narrow alleyways. A long time had passed since he had last been back to Santa Marta – four years, maybe. At first he had cut school to sneak up to the *favela*, meeting with his old friends and laughing about his new life. Eventually, tired of the arguments caused by Luiz slipping out, Ana had made him promise not to go back. She had a habit of making Luiz do things he didn't want to. Little sisters were like that, he grumbled to himself.

If Luiz had taken time to come to terms with their new life, Ana had fitted in seamlessly. Bubbly and popular, she had quickly caught up with her schoolwork and was soon outstripping her classmates. Earlier that very year, she had won the lead in the school play. Watching Ana up on the stage, Luiz felt he would burst with pride.

Now his sister had set her heart on becoming a journalist like their foster parents and was getting work experience at *O Globo*. In the last few weeks, Ana had been spending increasing amounts of time researching a piece she was hoping to show the editors at the newspaper. No matter how much Luiz teased her about her big 'scoop', she refused to talk about it. It was typical Ana – when she had her heart set on something, she went out and got it. Unlike her brother. God only knew what Luiz was going to do when he left school. He could just about keep up in class but was no rocket scientist – as Gui was quick to point out.

Luiz shook his head. Missing the beach for his sister's birthday was one thing, but his best friend would piss himself laughing if he could see Luiz pondering such deep thoughts.

Home was a detached house down a quiet residential street. As he turned the key in the front door, Luiz wasn't surprised to find that he had got back before Ana. He flicked on the television, then began rooting around in the fridge for something to eat. The news was still showing footage of the bus that had been held up two days ago, the camera focusing on the bloodstained window where Nene Barbosa had been killed. Something about this murder – the sheer senselessness of it – seemed to have shocked the city. Luiz could understand that. Only a month ago, he had watched Nene playing basketball for Flamengo, marvelling at the fact that the boy was only a year older than him. And now someone had shot him in the head.

The camera cut to a press conference on the steps of a police station. A bulky man in an expensive suit was standing in front of a bank of microphones, sweat glistening on top of his bald head.

'Councillor Cruz,' one of the reporters called out, 'I've been told that the police suspect the Barbosa murder was the work of the same gang responsible for the looting of the jewellery store in Ipanema – a gang calling themselves the Comando Negro. Can you confirm or deny these reports?'

The bald man held up his hands. 'The police are still carrying out their investigations and I'm not prepared to comment directly yet. What I will say is that – whatever name they call themselves – this pack of *favela* hoodlums has extinguished the life of one of Rio's most promising young men. Be assured that I will not rest until the animals responsible are in prison.'

Luiz shook his head. Councillor Jorge Cruz was always on the television bad-mouthing the *favelas*. He made it sound as though everyone who lived in the shanty towns was a member of a gang. Luiz's foster parents reckoned that there was something fishy about Cruz himself – his dad had investigated several shady business deals that had the councillor's fingerprints on them but could never prove anything. Not everyone in Rio had such a bad opinion of the *favelas*, but idiots like Cruz didn't help matters.

Luiz changed the channel to MTV and slumped down on the couch with a sandwich. He was dozing through an R&B video when he heard the front door open. Finally, Ana was back.

'You took your time,' he called out. 'You're late for your own party!'

'No one said anything about a party,' a man's voice replied.

Luiz sprang up from the sofa as three strangers walked casually into the room. Dressed in business suits, they carried themselves with the calm self-confidence of policemen. None of them bothered to flash any ID cards, however, and they had just walked uninvited into Luiz's house.

'Who are you?' he said.

'Nice place,' one of the men said conversationally, ignoring the question.

Shorter than his two companions, he was wearing dark sunglasses. He picked up a vase Luiz's mum had brought back from a trip to Europe and inspected it curiously.

'What do you want?' Luiz asked, his heart beating loudly.

'Just a chat. Nothing to get excited about,' the man replied. He glanced around the room. 'Perhaps here isn't the best place, though.'

'I can't go anywhere,' Luiz said, stalling. 'My sister's gone to the shops and she hasn't got a key.'

The man glanced up sharply and put down the vase. 'That's not a good start,' he said. 'All we want is a chat and already you're lying to us. Ana's not at the shops. What you should be asking yourself, Luiz, is – where is she?'

He knew their names. Luiz's blood froze.

'What do you mean, where is she? Is Ana all right? What have you done with her?'

'Such a lot of questions!' the man said, smiling. 'Why don't you come with us and we'll talk about it?'

'I'm not going anywhere until you tell me where Ana is,' Luiz replied stubbornly.

One of the other men clamped a hand down on Luiz's arm.

'Get moving, you little shit,' he said.

Luiz didn't even think about it. Instinctively he swung his left elbow into the man's face, felt his nose crumple on impact. The man cried out and staggered back, clutching his face. Immediately Luiz was on his toes, vaulting over the couch as the man with the sunglasses leaned over to grab him. As the third man raced to cut off the doorway, Luiz kicked him hard in the kneecap. He was rewarded by a loud curse and a clumsy punch thrown in his direction. Stepping neatly out of the way, Luiz caught the man on the side of the head with a punch of his own and watched him drop to the floor. Then he whirled round to take on his final assailant.

Too late.

The man with the sunglasses was standing right behind him, a black taser in his hand. He pressed the trigger, firing two darts through Luiz's clothes and into his skin. A sheet of white pain enveloped Luiz, and he screamed in agony as he fell to the floor. As he lay there, limbs trembling, unable to fight back, the man produced a cloth from his pocket and pressed it over Luiz's face. For a second he was overwhelmed by a sickly sweet smell and then everything went black.

3. Trojan Industries

Luiz came to, and immediately wished that he hadn't. There was a thundering pain in his head and a sour taste in his mouth. It felt as though someone had dropped an anvil on his skull.

Blearily, he took in his new surroundings. He was stretched out on a couch in a small office, the air conditioning humming softly above his head. The room was dominated by a burnished wooden desk, upon which a laptop lay open next to a jug of water. A row of filing cabinets ran the length of the left-hand wall, while a leafy plant pot had been positioned in the far right-hand corner. Through the blinds in the window, Rio's skyline was darkening with the onset of evening.

Struggling to sit upright, Luiz found himself face to face with a man in a chair that had been reversed so he could rest his arms upon its back. He was tall and black, wearing a crisp shirt and pinstriped trousers. A diamond stud gleamed in his left ear. Although no longer a young man – his short black hair was flecked with grey – he was well built, his clothes failing to disguise his muscular physique. The man watched Luiz intently through a pair of angular glasses.

'Headache?' he asked, in a deep American accent.

Luiz nodded, the motion sending shooting pains through his skull.

'My apologies. My men were told not to hurt you, but it appears you caught them off guard. You broke Freddie's nose.'

It was said matter-of-factly, without reproach. The man stood up and walked over to his desk, pouring a glass of water from a jug and handing it to Luiz.

'You pack quite a punch for a young man,' he continued. 'I'm guessing you've had some martial arts training?'

'Capoeira,' mumbled Luiz. 'My parents thought it would help my temper.'

'And did it?'

'Most of the time.' Luiz took a cautious sip of water. 'Where am I?'

'In my office. My name's Jordan. Darius Jordan.'

'What do you want with me?'

Jordan leaned against his desk, his steely gaze never wavering from Luiz.

'There was something I wanted to discuss with you. A business arrangement, if you will.'

Luiz gingerly touched the swollen bump on his head. 'You've got a funny way of doing business,' he said ruefully.

Jordan smiled, taking him by surprise. 'Not everything can be done by the book, Luiz. I should have thought you of all people would understand that.'

'What do you mean?'

'Let's just say I know more about you than you realize.'

Moving over to the filing cabinet, Jordan removed a large brown folder and began leafing through it.

'What's that?' Luiz asked curiously.

'You,' Jordan replied, pursing his lips as he scanned a piece of paper. 'This file contains the life history of Luiz Alves: birth certificate, adoption papers, arrest record . . .'

'Where did you get that?'

'You can get hold of anything if you ask the right people.' Jordan glanced up at Luiz. 'Do you know what I find interesting about this file? There are two different people here. The Luiz who lives in Botafogo now with his foster parents seems like a nice, quiet kid. Perhaps not the best at school, but he keeps his head down, doesn't cause any trouble.

'But then there's another Luiz, a younger kid who grew up in Santa Marta. He wasn't such an upstanding citizen. In fact, *that* Luiz was arrested several times – fighting, breaking and entering, even a car theft.'

'Hey!' Luiz protested. 'They couldn't prove anything on the car thing. They dropped the case.'

'Do you like cars, Luiz?'

Luiz shrugged, folding his arms obstinately. Jordan eye-balled him for a few seconds, then returned to his folder.

'So I was wondering, what happened here? Have you really gone straight, or have you just got smarter?'

'I don't do that sort of thing any more,' Luiz said. 'I promised my sister.'

'Ah, yes. Ana Alves.' Returning to the filing cabinet, Jordan pulled out an identical brown folder. 'There are no such skeletons in Ana's closet. Studies hard at school, good grades, community work . . .'

'She's a good kid,' Luiz said fiercely.

'Undoubtedly. Which makes her arrest all the more inexplicable.'

Luiz paused.

'Arrest?' he said quietly. 'What do you mean?'

'Last night police apprehended Ana in a car outside the Borel *favela*. They found half a kilo of cocaine in the boot. She's in custody now, on charges of drug possession and intent to supply.'

Luiz laughed incredulously. 'You're lying! Ana wouldn't touch drugs!'

'OK,' Jordan said mildly.

'I'm not listening to any more of this shit,' Luiz said, getting groggily to his feet. 'I'm out of here.'

'I understand completely,' Jordan replied smoothly. 'Though, if you don't believe me, you could always ask Ana yourself.'

He took out a slim mobile phone from his shirt pocket and tapped in a number. When a voice answered at the other end, Jordan wordlessly handed Luiz the mobile. The boy accepted it cautiously, handling the phone as though it were an unexploded bomb.

'Hello?' he said.

'Luiz?' a girl's voice replied. It was his sister. Usually breezy and ebullient, right now Ana sounded young and frightened. Her voice was echoing loudly, giving the impression she was in a very large room.

'Yeah – it's me. Where are you?'

'I don't know . . . a police station somewhere, I think. Luiz, I've made a terrible mistake.'

Luiz's heart sank as Ana's words came out in a sudden flood.

'I thought I needed a big story to impress the editors at *O Globo*, so I started digging around. There's a guy at Sacred Heart who's always boasting that he buys cocaine in the Borel *favela*, so I pretended to like him and we started hanging out. Last night we were supposed to be going to a party together, but just before we reached the warehouse he stopped the car and got out. He said he was only going to buy beer, but he didn't come back. The next thing I knew there were police everywhere. I told them I was working on a newspaper story, but they wouldn't listen to me. I didn't know that there were drugs in the boot, Luiz, I swear.' Ana suddenly paused. 'How did you find out about me?'

Luiz glanced up at Jordan. 'A friend told me. Look, are you OK?'

'I guess,' his sister replied. 'But they say they're going to charge me with drug dealing, that there's going to be a big court case and I'm going to go to prison, and I don't want to go to prison, Luiz. Mum and Dad are going to be so ashamed when they find out.'

With that, Ana broke into halting sobs.

'Don't worry about that now,' Luiz said soothingly. 'I'm going to do everything I can to sort this out.'

'What can you do?'

'I'm not sure yet. But there may be a way out of this. Don't talk to Mum and Dad until I get back to you, OK?'

'OK,' sniffed Ana. 'I'm sorry I dragged you into this. It's all my fault.'

'You are an *unbelievable* pain,' Luiz agreed, trying to sound upbeat. 'But then, you are my sister. I'll speak to you soon, OK? Look after yourself.'

He ended the call and handed the phone back to Jordan, his head spinning.

'So you were telling the truth,' Luiz said. 'Ana's in trouble. What do I do now?'

'What do you think you should do?'

'I dunno – go home, I guess, and call my parents. They're away at the moment, but they can get in touch with a lawyer.'

'Good plan,' said Jordan. 'That sounds like a very sensible course of action.'

'So I can just walk out of the door?' Luiz asked suspiciously. 'You'll let me go?'

Jordan laughed. 'Take the elevator down to the ground level. No one will stop you. You're not a hostage.' As Luiz made for the door, he called out, 'Although, if you do speak to your parents, it means I won't be able to free Ana.'

Luiz stopped in his tracks. 'You can do that?'

'Like I said,' Jordan said calmly, 'you can get anything you want – if you ask the right people.'

Luiz looked again around the neat office, bemused.

'What sort of business *is* this?'

'You're sitting in the main office of Trojan Industries. Here at Trojan, our business is very specific. We are interested in one thing and one thing only.'

'What's that?'

Jordan took off his glasses. 'Gangs,' he said.

'Gangs?' echoed Luiz.

'Trojan Industries is a shell, a facade. It pretends to be a multinational trading company, but in fact we're a covert operation. Our mission is to travel from country to country, infiltrating and bringing down the most vicious gangs in the world.'

'And you've come to Rio?'

Jordan gestured for Luiz to sit down again. 'You're a local boy. You know the deal. This is a beautiful city with a big problem: drugs. The drug market in Rio alone is worth around one hundred and fifty million dollars a year. That kind of money tends to attract the wrong sort of people, Luiz. Every day, gangs in the *favelas* fight and kill one another for the right to sell the drugs and to maintain control of their territories.'

None of this was news to Luiz. Baffled, he ran a hand across his forehead. 'What's this got to do with me and Ana?'

'You ever heard of a gang called the Comando Negro?'

'I guess,' Luiz said, shrugging. 'Saw that murder on the news the other day.'

'That's how they operate. Even by Rio's standards, this is one seriously violent gang. Wherever the Comando Negro goes, death follows. To make matters worse, somehow they've secured a way of transporting large amounts of cocaine into Rio, and it's good stuff. Now they're making a killing – literally. At this rate, they're going to become the biggest gang in the city.'

'And you want to stop them?'

Jordan nodded. 'Indeed I do. The problem is that nobody knows anything about them. They seem to have sprung up from nowhere, like some sort of killer virus. We've had snatches of information, but it's mostly hearsay and rumour – and we need cold, hard facts. The only thing we know for sure about the Comando Negro is that they're based in the Santa Marta *favela*.' Jordan tapped Luiz's file, his eyes narrowing. 'Where you grew up.'

'Wait a second,' Luiz said, the truth slowly dawning upon him. 'Are you saying you want me to go back to Santa Marta? And, what, spy on the Comando Negro?'

Jordan nodded deliberately.

Luiz laughed. 'That's crazy. You must be nuts.'

'I'm perfectly sane,' Jordan replied calmly. 'And perfectly serious.'

'Do you know what the gangs do to spies and informers? Haven't you heard about the microwave?'

Jordan raised an inquisitive eyebrow. 'Microwave?'

'They cut off your arms and legs,' said Luiz, 'while you're still alive. Then they cut off your head. Then they set fire to what's left. You think I want that to happen to me? I'm not going to spy for you, man.'

'I never said there wouldn't be risks, Luiz,' Jordan said seriously. 'Outside the *favela*, Trojan can provide you with all the technical support you'll need, but inside you'll be on your own.'

'And if I do this for you, you can get Ana out of custody?'

Jordan nodded.

'How do I know you're for real? Do it now. Get her out.'

'Much as I'd like to help your sister right now, this is business. You don't get anything for free, Luiz. But if you do agree to help us, we can arrange for her to be held in a cell on her own until your mission is complete. Give us the information that will bring down the Comando Negro and the charges against Ana will disappear.'

'But what about school? Our parents? Someone's going to find out what's going on.'

'Well, we know that your parents are in São Paulo for a fortnight, and we can organize things with your school so that the teachers don't ask any questions about you missing class. After that, it's up to you. Phone your parents whenever you want to. But remember, if you give the game away, I can promise you two things. One, you'll never see me again; and two, your sister will end up doing some serious jail time. Do we have a deal?'

Luiz blew the air from his cheeks. 'Doesn't look like I've got much of a choice,' he said finally.

'There's always a choice,' Jordan replied softly.

He slipped the phone back into his pockets and pressed an intercom buzzer on the desk. A slim, elegant woman, her hair scraped back into a tight ponytail, walked into the office. She sized up Luiz in one efficient glance.

'Luiz, this is Valerie Singer,' said Jordan. 'She's head of Human Resources here at Trojan. She'll fill you in on your mission details.'

'Come on,' the woman said crisply, in heavily accented English.

'Where are we going?'

'I'll tell you on the way.'

As he trailed out of the office after Singer, Luiz looked back over his shoulder. Jordan was still watching him. And, for the first time since they had met, Luiz saw a shadow of concern in his eyes.

4. Crash Course

As Valerie called the elevator in the hallway outside, Luiz's head was bursting with questions. There was so much to take in – too much, in fact. Part of him couldn't help wondering whether this was all some kind of elaborate practical joke. Something about the woman's brisk manner, however, told him that it was wise to keep his mouth shut for now. He stood in silence as the doors pinged open and the elevator purred down to the ground floor. There was no one in the large, marble-floored lobby – no receptionists behind the front desk, no security guards watching the doors. No one saw them leave.

Although it was early evening, the streets of Rio were still hot and humid. Luiz's school shirt clung damply to his back and his head was groaning in protest from the blow it had received. Outside the front of the building, a sleek white Mercedes with tinted windows was waiting for them. Scanning the street, Valerie opened the rear passenger door and gestured for Luiz to climb in. As she followed him, Luiz was surprised to see a pistol holster poking out from beneath her suit jacket. He bit back another question.

As the Mercedes pulled away from the side of the road, the identity of the driver hidden behind a partition, Valerie pulled out a packet of cigarettes and lit one. Soon the back seat was filled with acrid smoke. Trying not to cough, Luiz looked out of the window and saw that they were heading north out of the city. A police checkpoint was looming up in the middle of the road ahead of them, manned by burly officers dressed in black with M16 rifles hanging threateningly from their sides. Such checkpoints were a regular sight in Rio, but as one of the policemen waved at the car to halt, this time Luiz had to restrain himself from banging on the windows and screaming for help. Whatever trouble he was in, Ana was in deeper, and if Trojan could help her Luiz needed to be strong. Holding his breath, he heard the driver of the Mercedes roll down his window and murmur something at the policeman, who immediately waved the car through the roadblock.

They continued north along the coastline in the direction of Santos Dumont Airport, the sky darkening as the sun dipped behind the mountains. The road grew quieter, more desolate. Eventually the Mercedes drew to a halt in front of a large warehouse in the middle of an industrial complex that was cordoned off from the public by high iron railings. A lone, plain-clothed man stood guard by the gate, beside a battered sign that read TROJAN INDUSTRIES LTD.

At first glance, everything looked shabby and run-down, but then Luiz noticed the high-tech security cameras on top of the gates, swivelling from side to side to maintain a constant vigil over the surrounding area. As the Mercedes approached, the gates opened automatically, and when Valerie wound down the window and flashed an identification card at the guard, Luiz saw that the man was armed. There was more going on here than met the eye.

The warehouse itself was isolated in the centre of a vast wasteland, a castle in a flat kingdom of concrete. The kind of place where no one would hear you scream, Luiz thought glumly to himself. The car drove round the side of the building, stopping by a reinforced-steel door. Valerie got out of the back seat and pressed her palm against a pad built into the wall. There was a beep, then the steel door opened. Pausing in the doorway to beckon at Luiz, Valerie entered the building. Warily, the boy followed her inside.

Luiz found himself in a giant, gloomy space illuminated by powerful spotlights that hung down from the ceiling. To his left was a makeshift office, where workstations with blinking computer screens were separated by low partitions. The technology looked sophisticated, out of place in such a decrepit building. At the far side of the building, beyond a thick glass screen, Luiz saw a row of narrow passageways side by side. At first, ridiculously, he thought they were bowling alleys. It was only when he spotted the human-shaped targets at the end that he realized he was looking at a firing range.

'What *is* this place?' breathed Luiz.

'Trojan HQ,' Valerie replied. 'Until you go into the *favela*, this will be your home. You'll sleep here, eat here and train here.'

'Train? How long am I going to be here?'

'We're working on arranging a contact for you in the Comando Negro. You can't just stroll up into the *favela*. It could take a week, could take a couple of hours. When the call comes, you're going in. Here.'

She passed him a water bottle and pressed two small white tablets into his hand. Luiz looked at them dubiously.

'What are these?'

'Cyanide tablets. In case you get caught by the enemy.' Seeing the shocked look on his face, Valerie rolled her eyes. 'They're aspirin, Luiz. I'm guessing you've got a headache?'

'Oh,' Luiz said, feeling foolish. He took a swig from the water bottle and gulped the tablets back.

'The living quarters are upstairs,' said Valerie. 'I'll show you where you're sleeping.'

Trailing along in Valerie's wake, Luiz felt suddenly weary. Only a few hours ago he had been sitting at home waiting for his sister's birthday party. Now Ana was in jail and he was stuck with this strange, icy woman in the middle of nowhere. If he hadn't been numb with shock, it would have felt like a nightmare.

Valerie walked up a staircase, her heels clicking on the metal steps, and along a raised walkway. She led Luiz past a series of numbered doors with small, circular windows set into them. As far as Luiz could tell, there was no one else up here.

At Room 5, they stopped. Valerie pushed the door

open, revealing a small room with a bed, a basin and mirror, and a wardrobe. Luiz sat down on the bed, his muscles heavy. He failed to stifle a jaw-breaking yawn.

'Why do I feel so tired?' he muttered.

Valerie shrugged. 'Those tablets weren't aspirin. They were sleeping pills.'

'You drugged me?' Luiz said drowsily, struggling to focus. 'Why?'

'We've got a lot to get through tomorrow. You're going to need your wits about you. Enough questions for now. Sleep.'

The last thing Luiz saw – before he was knocked unconscious for the second time in a matter of hours – was Valerie's face staring grimly down at him.

If Luiz needed time to come to terms with what had happened to him, it soon became clear that Trojan wasn't going to give it to him. There wasn't even time to blink. The next day he was abruptly shaken awake by Valerie, who waited outside while Luiz groggily came to, then washed in the basin and pulled on the clothes he found folded up in the wardrobe. Although he guessed that it was early morning, he couldn't be sure. There were no clocks on the walls, no windows, no way of telling whether it was night or day. The warehouse seemed to run on its own time.

After a quick breakfast of fruit and coffee in a deserted canteen, he was led by Valerie to the makeshift office, which was now occupied by a group of people working at their computers. A tall white man perched casually on the edge of a table, humming tunelessly to himself. He smiled as Luiz approached.

'Luiz, meet Richard Madison,' said Valerie. 'He's head of Technical Support at Trojan and he'll be responsible for your training. Madison's ex-SIS, the British intelligence agency, and has hunted for Al-Qaeda members in the mountains of Pakistan.' She leaned in closely. 'So, if I were you, I'd listen to him.'

Nodding briefly at Madison, Valerie turned on her heel and walked away. Luiz watched her go.

'She's friendly,' he said sourly.

A grin broke out on Madison's face – the first smile Luiz had seen for what felt like an age. 'Don't take it personally, lad,' he said, in English. 'Valerie's like that with everyone. Not a lot of call for jokes in Mossad.'

Luiz gave him a blank look.

'Israeli secret service,' the British man explained. 'And, believe me, what those guys lack in humour, they make up for in expertise.'

Luiz remembered the gun holster he had seen Valerie wearing the previous evening. He glanced around the bustling office. 'Did *everyone* here used to be in the military?'

Madison nodded. 'Trojan wouldn't stand much of a chance otherwise. Over the years Darius has built up enough contacts to put a team together.'

'And was he . . .?'

'Ex-Delta Force – American special forces. There are very few front lines where that man hasn't seen action.

31

He's been to places that make my tours look like Disney-land.'

Thinking back to their meeting in his office, Luiz remembered Jordan's powerful build, the clipped authority of his movements. Perhaps it wasn't that surprising after all.

Madison looked at him thoughtfully. 'So I'm guessing you've had a bloody strange few hours.'

'Yeah, you could say that.'

'I'm afraid that's the way it's got to be. If the Brazilian government find out what we're doing here, the shit's going to hit the fan and no mistake. We've got to stay under the radar – get in and get out, like a commando raid. We haven't really got the time to explain things over a cup of tea.'

'I don't get it,' Luiz said. 'If the government doesn't know about you, what are you doing here?'

Madison frowned. 'Have you ever heard of the term "black op"?'

Luiz shook his head.

'It describes military operations that are too risky – or too shady – for governments to back openly. They may know something's going on, but they'll deny it if you ask them. As it happens, several senior officials in Interpol know about us, but we're on a kind of probation. This is our first mission, and you're our first recruit, Luiz. If there's a cock-up here, you'll also be our last.'

Madison was interrupted by his bleeper chirping into life. He consulted the electronic readout.

'I have to call someone. Hang on a second.'

The Brit hurried away, leaving Luiz standing on his own in the office. None of the computer operatives had given him a second glance. Bored, Luiz looked about the warehouse, his eyes catching sight of a side door resting invitingly ajar. Glancing around to check that nobody was watching him, he crept over to the door and slipped outside.

After the claustrophobia of Trojan's warehouse, it was a relief to be standing in the sunshine again. As Luiz took deep gulps of fresh air, his eyes alighted upon a classic red Corvette parked nearby, its bodywork gleaming in the sunlight. Staring at the car's smooth contours, Luiz felt a familiar, irresistible urge.

If Trojan wanted a secret agent, they'd get one.

He ran across to the car and, finding one of the doors open, slipped into the driver's seat. Reaching down beneath the dashboard, Luiz teased out the wiring. Although he hadn't admitted it to Darius Jordan, he had stolen his first car back in Santa Marta and had quickly grown to love speeding around in other people's flash machines. Having promised Ana to go straight, several years had elapsed since Luiz had last hotwired a car and he felt a surge of elation when the engine burst into life. He revved the engine, feeling the steering wheel tremble with anticipation beneath his grasp.

In his rear-view mirror, Luiz saw Richard Madison appear in the warehouse doorway. Instinctively, he stamped down on the accelerator. The Corvette screamed away across the concrete, the force of the acceleration pinning Luiz back against the seat. He laughed, exhilarated by the awesome speed of the machine. As the perimeter fence hurtled towards him, he waited until the last second and then spun the steering wheel, veering back towards open ground.

For five minutes Madison looked on, arms folded, as Luiz threw the Corvette into a series of wide, skidding rings, smoke billowing from its screaming tyres. The Brit waited patiently until Luiz had brought the car to a screeching halt, then strolled over and tapped on the window. Luiz had the distinct feeling that Madison was trying to hide a grin.

He pressed the window button down.

'If you've buggered up my car, sonny,' Madison said, 'I'll wring your bloody neck.'

Luiz gave him a beaming smile. 'It's safe with me,' he said. 'Didn't Jordan tell you? I like cars.'

5. Sure Shot

The next couple of days passed by in a blur for Luiz. He was thrown into a series of intensive lessons that made school look like easy street. There was a lot to go over before he could return to the *favela* and Trojan Industries were nothing if not thorough. Luiz was allowed breaks only to eat and sleep. Thankfully, no one tried to give him any more 'aspirin'. They didn't need to – Luiz was so shattered he fell asleep immediately.

However, life under the tutelage of the easy-going Richard Madison wasn't all bad. To Luiz's immense relief, Valerie had faded into the background, allowing the former SIS man to supervise his training. Occasionally, sitting at a computer screen, Luiz would feel the hairs on the back of his neck stand up and he'd turn round to find the Israeli woman watching him. She never said a word, though.

To his surprise, most of Luiz's time was taken up with language lessons. One of Trojan's operatives, a young Brazilian guy called Ricardo, was teaching him *favela* slang. Four years in the suburbs had changed Luiz's vocabulary and softened his accent. If he walked into Santa Marta talking like a rich kid, there was no way the Comando Negro were going to accept him as a gang member. It didn't take long for Luiz to remember the language and his old accent soon began to return.

As his voice changed, so did his appearance. Luiz's curly black hair was shaved off, leaving him with a skinhead. Temporary tattoos were pressed on to his arms, leaving them banded with ornate circular patterns that to his eyes looked indistinguishable from the real thing. Luiz spent time staring at himself in the mirror, getting used to his new look and trying to adopt the surly, assertive body language of the gang members.

One afternoon Richard Madison beckoned Luiz away from his workstation and led him towards the firing range on the other side of the warehouse.

'I've been talking to Darius,' the Brit began, 'and apparently we don't need to worry about you getting involved in any hand-to-hand fighting. I hear you've been trained in capoeira.'

'I can look after myself,' Luiz said cautiously.

'That's good to hear. You've got enough on your plate right now without having to learn how to fight too. However, there is one thing that I do need to show you.'

Madison stopped by the transparent plastic door at the end of the firing range and pressed his palm against the reader. The door clicked open and he stepped inside. In the walkway beyond, a small arsenal of pistols and semi-automatic rifles had been laid out along a table. As Luiz looked over the array of weaponry, the metal gleaming slickly in the light, the dangerous reality of what he was doing suddenly hit home.

'You're going to give me a gun?'

'Not if we can possibly avoid it,' Madison replied. 'But the Comando Negro are going to be armed and it's better that you know what you're doing. Less chance of you hurting yourself, or anyone else. I'm guessing you've never fired a gun before.'

Luiz shook his head.

'Well, here's your chance.' He selected a small black pistol and handed it to Luiz, who was surprised at how heavy it felt in his hand.

'This is a Glock 26,' Madison said. 'It's Austrian-made, reliable and accurate. The 26s are standard issue for policemen here in Rio.'

Instructing Luiz to put on a pair of ballistic ear defenders and safety goggles, the Brit led him over to the range. At the other end of the alleyway, the outline of a man had been drawn on a white target. Madison crisply showed Luiz how to load a magazine into the Glock and then pointed at the target.

'Do your worst,' he said.

Taking a deep breath, Luiz aimed at the target and squeezed the trigger. Unprepared for the recoil of the gun, he stumbled backwards, shockwaves running up his right arm. The sound of the gunshot echoed around the firing range.

'Wow!' shouted Luiz, peering at the target. 'Did I hit anything?'

Madison gave him a sideways glance. 'You were closer to hitting me than the bad guy, but never mind. Try it again. Keep your right arm straight this time and your left arm slightly bent. And you want to shoot side-on, with your left foot pointing towards the target. Fire face-on and you'll present more of a target to anyone that wants to shoot back.'

Bracing himself, Luiz fired again. This time he managed to maintain his stance and saw to his satisfaction that he had clipped the edge of the white target.

'Better?' he said.

Madison nodded, a flicker of amusement on his face.

As time passed, Luiz had to admit that there was something darkly exhilarating about shooting a gun. The first time he hit a clean shot in the centre of the target's head, he felt a small surge of triumph. After an hour, his arms were aching and his ears were ringing, but he was regularly hitting the target. Seemingly satisfied by his progress, Madison called a halt to the session.

'Not bad,' he said approvingly.

Luiz grinned. 'More fun than I thought it would be.'

'It might be fun in here, Luiz,' Madison said seriously, 'but when you get on the outside it's a whole different ball game.' He took the Glock from Luiz's hands and put it back on the table. 'Like I said, let's pray you never have to use one for real.'

For Luiz, the firearms lesson was the most vivid moment of a surreal few days. In a way, it was good that he was busy learning so much. He didn't want time to sit down and think what was happening to him. Here in the warehouse everything made a strange sort of sense. His one contact with the outside world was his mobile phone, which, to his surprise, Trojan had allowed him to keep. Luiz had received several texts from Gui, checking to see if he was OK. It turned out that Trojan had concocted a story that Luiz and Ana had been called away on a family emergency and would be missing from school for a couple of weeks. It had taken all of Luiz's self-control not to phone his best friend back and tell him the truth. But he knew that if word got out, then Ana would have to stay in custody. Anyway, Gui would probably just think he was bullshitting. Luiz couldn't quite believe what was going on himself.

Worse than that was the phone call he had received from his foster parents. When his mum asked him about Ana, he said that she had lost her phone and that she was out shopping. As hard as he tried to sound cheerful, Luiz hated lying to them. Once he had put the phone down, he made an effort to put them out of his mind. Thinking about them only upset him and, for Ana's sake, he couldn't fall apart now.

'So you want to join the Comando Negro, kid?' the boy sneered. 'Sure, no problem. Only one little thing. *We don't take spies.*'

'But I'm telling you, I'm not a spy!' Luiz shouted.

He was lying spread-eagled on a patch of wasteland, his arms and legs pinned to the ground by a pack of boys dressed in black. They were laughing and taunting him as he tried to struggle free.

'You know what happens to spies, don't you?' The gang leader leaned in closer. 'They get put in the microwave . . .'

'No!' Luiz gasped. 'Please! I'm not a spy! You have to believe me!'

As the gang leader produced a small hacksaw from his belt, Luiz tried to writhe free, but his muscles felt as weak as a baby's. He was utterly helpless. When he felt the saw bite into his legs, he started screaming . . .

Luiz awoke with a start, springing bolt upright in bed. A nightmare. It had felt so real. He was panting and his chest was drenched with sweat. He rubbed his face with his hands and waited for his breathing to calm down.

Luiz hopped out of bed, pulled on a T-shirt and went in search of a glass of water. As he padded barefoot outside his room, he saw that the warehouse spotlights had been dimmed and the cavernous building was deserted. The only sound was the whirring of computer processors. Lights blinked on digital maps like fireflies.

Luiz was making his way to the canteen when he heard the sound of voices coming from a conference room, one of which was the rich, unmistakable baritone of Darius Jordan. Luiz had never seen inside the conference room before, but now the door was slightly open, a crack of light spilling out into the warehouse. Keeping tight to the wall, Luiz crept over to the door and pressed his ear against it.

'So,' he heard Jordan say, 'give me a progress report. How's our boy shaping up?'

'Better than expected,' Richard Madison replied. 'He was a bit shell-shocked at first, but he's got spirit. Asks sensible questions and picks things up quickly. And you were right about cars, Darius. I set it up so he had a chance to give my Corvette the once-over and he didn't need a second invitation. Put him behind the wheel and he turns into Lewis bloody Hamilton. We have to use this. If Luiz walks up to the Comando Negro and says he wants to be a soldier, they'll laugh at him. And then probably shoot him. If they need a driver, on the other hand . . .'

'What about you, Valerie?'

There was a pause, then Singer replied. 'Another couple of months' training and maybe he's OK. You send in him now and he won't last a day. Luiz simply isn't tough enough yet.'

'You starting to get all maternal towards the lad?' Madison asked slyly.

There was an icy pause.

'I don't like waste,' replied Valerie.

'Ready or not, now's the time,' another man said. He sounded local, speaking English with a thick Portuguese accent. 'I came here tonight because we've got a contact Luiz can use. But that's not the point.'

'Then what is?' asked Jordan.

'Darius, you know how much I respect you,' the local man continued. 'I wouldn't be here otherwise. But whether you start tomorrow or in a month's time, this mission is still insane! Do you have any idea what you're sending that kid into? What sort of danger he's in?'

'I am aware of what we're asking him,' Jordan replied calmly.

'I've been up against the *favela* gangs for twenty years now,' the new man continued, 'but I haven't seen anything like the Comando Negro before. They're organized, well financed and utterly ruthless. It's a nasty combination, Darius.'

'I know. That's why we're here.'

'But he's just a kid!'

'If I could go in there, I would,' Jordan replied. 'But a forty-five-year-old American isn't exactly going to blend in. We've talked about this, Juan. This is the only way we can stop these gangs.'

'I still say it's crazy.'

Luiz had heard enough. He pushed the door open and strode into the room. Jordan, Madison, Singer and another man were sitting around a circular table. On the back of the wall was a large map of Santa Marta *favela*. As Luiz entered the room, three of them looked up, startled. Only Jordan seemed unsurprised.

'Anyone want to know what I think?' Luiz said.

Jordan pressed the tips of his fingers together thought-fully. 'Seems only fair. After all, you've heard what we think. Do you need more time for training? Or are you ready to go into Santa Marta now?'

'My sister's sitting in a prison cell and she's not going anywhere until I do this mission for you.' Luiz glanced defiantly at Valerie Singer. 'You're damn right I'm ready to go in.'

'Well, then, I guess you'd better sit down.'

As Luiz pulled up a chair, Jordan gestured at the new man. 'This is Juan Oliveira. He's a policeman here in Rio. Trojan uses him as an outside consultant. No one knows the *favelas* better than him.'

Oliveira must have been about the same age as Jordan. He was a large man with tanned skin and piercing blue eyes. He was wearing a leather jacket over a white T-shirt. Luiz looked at him mistrustfully. Even in the middle-class suburbs of Rio, policemen tended to be treated with suspicion. There were rumours of corruption, brutality, kidnappings – even murders.

'You can trust him,' Richard Madison said quickly. 'Juan's one of the good guys.'

'A rare breed, I know,' Oliveira said. 'Good to meet you, Luiz.'

'Juan came here tonight because he's got a tip-off that we can use.'

Oliveira passed a photograph across the table to Luiz. It was a mugshot of a heavy-set teenager staring dully into the camera.

'Who's this?'

'Goes by the name of MC Livio. He's a *baile-funk* legend in Santa Marta.'

Luiz nodded. Though he hadn't heard of Livio, he knew all about *baile funk* – dance music with thick, looping basslines and harsh beats. Riotous *baile-funk* parties were held in halls and warehouses across the *favelas*, attracting kids from all over Rio in search of late-night fun.

'As far as I know,' Oliveira said, 'Livio's a recent recruit to the Comando Negro. He's a popular guy up in Santa Marta and he knows everyone in the *favela*. If anyone can get you into the gang, it's this kid. And it just so happens that we arrested him earlier tonight. He's sitting in a downtown jail cell, just waiting for you to introduce yourself.'

Jordan leaned forward. 'The more the Comando Negro build a name for themselves, the more territory they control, the more bodies they rack up, the harder the other gangs are going to come after them. They're going to need numbers sooner rather than later. Make a good impression on Livio and you've got a shot at infiltrating the Comando Negro. Make *that* happen and you can give us the information we need. Who's in charge of these guys, how they operate.' He paused. 'How we can bring them down.'

Luiz snorted. 'That's all?'

'That's the deal. That's what it'll take to get Ana out.'

'And I start with this guy Livio? Any idea how I make a good impression on him?'

Jordan smiled grimly. 'Leave that to us.'

6. First Contact

Early the next morning an unmarked police car entered the industrial complex and headed towards Trojan Industries' warehouse. Although the sun had only just begun to climb in the sky, it was already baking hot, a warm breeze whipping across the concrete. It was going to be a sweltering day.

Standing waiting in the warehouse doorway, Luiz bounced up and down on his toes like a boxer before a title fight. Too wired to sleep after his conversation with Jordan, he had spent the rest of the night pacing up and down in his room. With the adrenalin still coursing through his system, Luiz felt more awake and alert than ever.

Beside him, Richard Madison smiled.

'Take it easy, lad. Don't want to tire yourself out before you get there.'

'No chance of that,' Luiz replied. 'I'm buzzing.'

As the police car came to a halt beside them, the British man clasped Luiz's hand warmly and patted him on the shoulder.

'Here,' he said. 'Have this.'

Madison pressed a small, golden crucifix on a chain into Luiz's hands.

'Thanks,' Luiz said. 'I'm going to need it.'

'In more ways than you know. This crucifix has got a GPS tracker inside it. Wherever you go, we'll be able to follow you. Also, if you press the ends of both arms together, it'll send out an electronic distress signal. The cavalry will get there as soon as they can.'

'Let's hope I'm still alive by the time they arrive,' Luiz said gloomily.

Madison laughed. 'Take care of yourself out there. You'll do us proud, I know it.'

Looking at the affable Brit, Luiz realized that he was going to miss him.

'Leaving without saying goodbye?'

Which was not something Luiz could say about Valerie Singer. The Israeli woman had stolen up soundlessly behind him and was eyeing him with arch amusement through a large pair of sunglasses.

'Didn't think you'd miss me,' he replied in a surly tone of voice.

'No, maybe not,' agreed Valerie. 'But I'm coming with you anyway. I have some business in town.'

She sat down in the front passenger seat and promptly lit another cigarette. Luiz clambered into the back, where Juan Oliveira gave him a sombre nod. The policeman didn't seem any happier than he had at the meeting the night before. As the car pulled away, Luiz saw Madison wave farewell and then move back inside the warehouse. Of Trojan's head, Darius Jordan, there was no sign.

At this time of the morning, the coastal road was quiet

and the journey south back into the centre of Rio didn't take long. As they entered the heart of the city, Oliveira turned to Luiz.

'OK, so remember what we discussed last night. The plan is for you and Livio to get out in two days – I'll give you the signal when we're ready to go. This is pretty risky stuff and I want to make sure everything's in place before we run through it. You've got until then to get to know Livio. A word of advice: don't push it. Don't ask too many questions. These kids spend so much time smoking dope that they're all pretty paranoid. He needs to be sure you're his kind of guy.'

'Easier said than done,' muttered Luiz.

'It might not be as difficult as you think.' The policeman smiled. 'Remember, you've done a very bad thing and angered an important man . . .'

'We're nearly there,' Valerie rapped from the front seat. 'Cuff him.'

'What?' Luiz said, startled.

'It's going to look a bit strange if you walk into the police station like minor royalty. Better off you look like a proper gang member.' She stubbed out her cigarette in the front-seat ashtray. 'It starts here, Luiz. Time to go to work.'

As the car stopped outside a police station in the Zona Sul, Oliveira produced a pair of handcuffs from his pocket and snapped them around Luiz's wrists, the metal biting into his skin. The policeman hauled Luiz out of the back and pushed him up the steps, all traces of amiability gone.

Valerie Singer followed them through the glass entrance-way and into the cool hall beyond. Even though it was dark inside, she kept her sunglasses on.

'Got another VIP for the penthouse,' Oliveira called out to a policeman at the reception desk, clipping Luiz round the back of the head. 'Need someone to take him down to the cells.'

'Before you do,' Valerie cut in, 'there's something I need to show him. You can stay here.'

Without waiting for Oliveira's reply, she pushed Luiz past reception, taking him down a long, straight corridor. The room at the end was narrow and dark, dominated by a floor-length window that ran across one wall and looked out on to a second, brighter room. Through the window, Luiz saw a girl sitting at a table.

It was Ana.

Luiz's sister looked pale and drawn. There were dark circles beneath her eyes. Her clothes were grimy and her long hair was tangled, but Luiz was relieved to see that there were no marks or bruises on her skin. He banged on the window, calling out her name. Ana didn't turn round.

'She won't see or hear you,' Valerie said in his ear. 'It's a two-way mirror and the room's sound-proofed.'

'Let me go in and see her!'

Valerie shook her head. 'Not possible yet, I'm afraid. Perhaps in a couple of days. *After* you've spent some time in Santa Marta.'

'If I can't talk to her, why did you bring me here?' Luiz asked, between clenched teeth.

'Consider it a gentle reminder – just in case you were having second thoughts about the mission. We're doing all we can for Ana, but until you fulfil your side of the bargain, she's going nowhere.'

'You're a bitch,' Luiz spat.

'I've been called worse,' Valerie replied calmly. 'Livio's in one of the cells on the other side of the building. A guard will come and take you there in a few minutes. You can watch your sister until then.' She tucked a packet of cigarettes and a lighter into the breast pocket of Luiz's shirt and tapped his cheek.

'For making friends,' she said.

Valerie walked out of the observation room and locked the door behind her. Luiz hammered on the window, shouting until he was hoarse, but Ana didn't respond. At one point she turned and looked right at him, forlornly trying to rearrange her hair in the mirror, but there was no sign of recognition in her eyes.

He was still raging with frustration when the door was unlocked and a guard entered the room. If the man knew Luiz wasn't a real criminal, he hid it well. He roughly manhandled Luiz down to the basement, taking him to the end of a dingy row of cells, where a boy was stretched out on a bench, hands crossed behind his head.

MC Livio was dark-skinned with a pudgy face, clad in a voluminous basketball shirt that nearly reached his knees. A black baseball cap was set casually on his head. He looked up warily through heavy-lidded eyes as the guard unlocked Luiz's handcuffs and shoved him inside the cell. The cell door closed with a bang behind him.

'Bastards!' Luiz screamed, kicking one of the walls. His nostrils were flooded with a stench of sweat and urine.

'Quit yelling!' growled Livio. 'They like it if you do that. And you'll give me a headache.' The MC looked over at Luiz menacingly. 'Sit down and shut up.'

Luiz glared back, unwilling to give way too easily. Then he slammed his fist against the wall and slumped to the floor. Shaking his head, Livio lay back down on the bench, where he promptly dozed for hours, his chest rising and falling with every snore. There was a faint smell of marijuana among the acrid odours in the cell – Luiz guessed that the MC had been stoned when he was picked up and was now sleeping off the after-effects. As the morning dragged on into the afternoon and then the evening, Luiz remembered Oliveira's advice and sat in silence, waiting patiently for his moment. There was no way he was going to speak first.

When night fell, the harsh strip lights in the cell suddenly flicked off without the two boys exchanging another word.

As morning broke over the police station, Luiz woke up with his joints stiff from the hard floor. He stood up and stretched, to find Livio staring at him, as though the MC was weighing something up. Eventually Livio nodded at him.

'So where you from, then?'

Luiz shrugged. 'Around.'

'Around? What's that mean? You gotta be from *somewhere*, man.'

'Last place I was in was Rocinha. Before that Borel. Before that, somewhere else. I don't stick around places very long. What about you?'

Livio leaned back on his bench. 'Santa Marta,' he said, casually tapping his black baseball cap. 'I run with the Comando Negro.'

'Really?' Luiz raised an eyebrow. 'I heard about them. Fierce reputation.'

'Better believe it,' Livio replied meaningfully.

The MC seemed more inclined to talk now and the two boys began a cautious exchange. It wasn't long before the conversation turned to football and to Luiz's relief he discovered that they were both fans of the same club: Botafogo. The boys commiserated with one another over their poor season and the recent defeat by arch-rivals Fluminense. Slowly, Livio's hostile manner began to soften, giving Luiz a glimpse of a more open character beneath the bluster.

Midway through the morning, they were interrupted by a commotion in the corridor outside. Juan Oliveira was marching a handcuffed prisoner past their cage. At the sight of Luiz, the man's eyes bulged and he broke away towards them.

'You little shit!' he screamed. 'I heard what you did! I'm going to kill you! You're a marked man!'

As the man ranted and raged at Luiz, the police guard

struggled to wrestle him away from the cell. Finally the angry prisoner was led away down the corridor, leaving a trail of abuse behind him as he went.

'Hey, I know that guy!' Livio said, scrambling to his feet and peering through the bars. 'He's the *dono* of a gang down in Rocinha! What the hell did you do to him?'

'I borrowed his car,' Luiz replied matter-of-factly. 'Had a little accident in it. That's why I'm here.'

'You stole a *dono*'s car? What make was it?'

'BMW convertible.'

Livio let out a low whistle. 'No wonder he's pissed. Why didn't you just run for it when you crashed the car?'

'There was a problem,' said Luiz. 'I crashed into a police car.'

Livio stared at him for a second, then burst out laughing. The MC reached across and slapped Luiz on the back.

'I'd have loved to see the look on those bastards' faces! Almost worth ending up in here for.'

'What about you?' asked Luiz. 'Why are you here?'

'The usual bullshit.' Livio scratched his crotch, not bothering to explain further. 'I gotta go to court tomorrow. With my record, I'm screwed. Man, I could do with a smoke.'

Luiz produced the cigarette packet and lighter Valerie had given him and offered the MC one. He glanced up with surprise.

'You sure?'

'Keep the packet.'

'Really?'

'I'm trying to quit,' Luiz replied.

The MC snorted with amusement, secreting the cigarette packet within the folds of his basketball shirt. The day passed more quickly after that. Luiz wasn't sure if he had managed to gain Livio's trust, but at least the MC no longer looked like he wanted to punch him. Livio might have been a bit flabby, but Luiz wouldn't have wanted to get into a fight with him.

As the lights in the cell snapped off for the second night, the two of them settled down to go to sleep.

'So say you manage to avoid jail,' Livio said, a drowsy note creeping into his voice. 'What are you going to do then?'

Luiz shrugged. 'You heard the *dono* earlier. I sure as hell can't go back to Rocinha.' He paused. 'You reckon anyone in Santa Marta might need a driver?'

'What, like the Comando Negro? You serious?'

'I got to do something for money. Driving's all I know.'

The MC had a doubtful look on his face. 'I don't know, man. You've got balls, but we're taking it to a whole new level.'

'But if we could get out of here,' Luiz persisted, 'would you take me up to Santa Marta? Put a word in for me?'

'We get out of here, you can sleep with my sister,' grunted Livio.

With that, the MC's breathing became deeper and more even as he fell fast asleep. Luiz lay awake for hours, thinking, until finally exhaustion overtook him and he drifted off into a dreamless sleep.

7. Hell Mouth

They were brutally awoken by a policeman banging on the cage with his baton.

'Wake up, girls,' he shouted. 'Time to go to your prom!'

Livio rubbed his eyes sleepily and groaned. 'Man, I was having the nicest dream! I was with this beautiful girl and . . .'

The policeman strode over to the bench and dragged Livio to the floor.

'OK, OK!' the MC cried out, as the policeman raised his baton in the air. 'I'm up! No need to beat the shit out of me!'

The two boys were handcuffed and marched out of the cells. As they walked back through the main hallway, Luiz saw Juan Oliveira leaning on the reception desk.

'Have a nice day, girls,' he called out as they passed. 'Don't worry – there'll be lots of men in prison to keep you warm.'

'Go screw yourself,' Luiz spat back.

Oliveira whirled round and punched him in the belly, knocking the air from his lungs. As the policeman wrestled him to the ground, Luiz felt him press a metal key into his palm.

'You little scumbag,' Oliveira snarled in his ear. 'You'd better hope I don't see you again.'

He hauled Luiz to his feet and shoved him back to the guard.

'Get them out of my sight.'

Winded, Luiz staggered through the glass entrance alongside Livio and into the sunshine on the station steps. He had barely registered the police van waiting by the side of the road when a gunshot rang out.

The sound shattered the bright blue morning as though it were glass. There was a shocked pause, a second when everything froze and utter silence reigned. Then another gunshot rang out and all hell broke loose.

Passers-by began screaming, throwing themselves to the ground and covering their heads. Swearing, the policeman next to Luiz pushed him to one side and pulled a gun from his holster. He fired off a couple of return shots, aiming at a battered Ford on the other side of the street. There was a movement from behind the bonnet of the car and suddenly a third bullet flew narrowly past Luiz, smashing the Perspex doors of the police station with an earsplitting crash.

Grabbing the sluggish form of Livio, Luiz dived to his left, hunkering down behind the low wall that ran around the front of the police station.

'What the hell's going on?' the MC shouted.

'Search me!' Luiz yelled back. 'Guess someone hates the cops more than we do.'

Glancing around, he saw the policeman had taken cover behind the wall on the other side of the steps. From time to time the officer darted up from his cover to fire off intermittent shots, his attention fixed firmly on the mystery gunman behind the Ford. Producing the key Oliveira had stuffed into his hand, Luiz freed himself from his cuffs and then passed the key to Livio. The MC gave him a look of astonishment.

'How did you . . .?'

'Took it from the policeman when the shots began. Hurry up!'

As Livio fumbled to undo the lock, Luiz peered over the wall and saw what he was looking for: a white scooter handily parked in front of the police van. Just where Oliveira had promised it would be.

'Let's make a break for that bike,' he said.

'Are you crazy?' Livio hissed. 'It's a firefight out there.'

'Do you *want* to go to prison?' Luiz asked. 'Come on!'

He waited for a break in the shooting, then scrambled to his feet and jumped over the wall on to the pavement. Using the police van as cover, he crawled over to the scooter, then gestured frantically for Livio to follow. The MC seemed reluctant, but after a final look around him he hurriedly shambled over to the police van.

Policemen were pouring out on to the station steps – reinforcements had finally arrived. It was now or never. Luiz dashed out into the open and leaped on to the scooter.

'Get on!' he screamed at Livio.

As the MC bundled on to the back of the scooter, Luiz revved the handle and spurred the bike into life. With a roar it sped off down the road. There was a shout from the policemen behind them, then Luiz heard a bullet whiz over his head. He bent lower over the handlebars of the scooter and began zigzagging down the street, trying to present a difficult target. As they veered around a blue saloon, there was a pinging sound as a bullet hit the boot of the car.

'Holy shit!' Livio screamed. 'Let's move!'

Luiz didn't need to be told twice. He jammed down on the handle, urging the bike forward until it reached top speed, and the sound of gunfire fell away into the background.

From his vantage point in the doorway of the police station, Juan Oliveira watched the two boys speed off. As they disappeared from sight, the boy on the back of the scooter whooped, raising his middle finger in the air at the policemen. Oliveira waited for a few seconds, then stepped out into the open and held up his hand. The gunshots abruptly stopped, leaving the street in a state of dazed aftershock.

A man got up from behind the battered Ford and jogged over to Oliveira, stuffing his pistol back in his holster. Oliveira looked pointedly at the shattered door behind him.

'I don't recall telling you to destroy any doors, sergeant,' he said mildly.

'Sorry about that, sir,' the sergeant said. 'I pulled my shot to the left. What are you going to tell the bosses?'

'Guess I'll have to think of something.'

'Apart from that, it went according to plan,' the sergeant continued hastily. 'We did as you ordered – put on a bit of a show. Would have looked real enough to a civilian. But short of giving the little shits directions, we couldn't have made it any easier for them to escape. They'll be back in the *favela* before you know it.'

'Good.'

An uneasy look crossed the sergeant's face.

'This doesn't feel right, sir. Helping the bastards get away. You sure you can't tell me what this is about?'

Oliveira shook his head. The sergeant sighed. 'This is crazy, boss.'

'You're telling me,' Oliveira replied grimly, looking out in the direction of the boys.

As the motorbike careered through the streets of Rio, Livio laughed and hollered in Luiz's ear, shouting out insults about the police. Even though Luiz was focused on navigating the scooter through the traffic at breakneck speed, he couldn't deny the wave of elation that was washing over him. Despite the fact that Oliveira had explained exactly how the set-up would work back at Trojan's warehouse, it hadn't made the gunfight feel any less real.

Livio tapped him on the shoulder.

'Hey, let me off here,' he shouted, above the growl of the scooter's engine. 'There's something I gotta do.'

'What about the police?' Luiz shouted back, as they pulled up alongside a row of shops.

Livio shrugged. 'If they come after me, they come after me. I got bigger worries than them.'

'You want me to come with you?'

'Nah – you can get out of here.'

As the MC turned to leave, Luiz quickly called him back. 'Hey, wait! You just going to leave me here? You said you'd put a word in for me with the Comando Negro!'

'I don't know, Luiz,' Livio replied, looking suddenly uncertain. 'This might be a bad time. There's a lot of shit going down right now.'

'Come on, man! You promised!'

Luiz held his breath as Livio bit his lip in thought. Eventually, the MC nodded.

'OK. You know the way to Santa Marta?'

Luiz nodded.

'I'll meet you at the *boca* in an hour. No promises, though.' He exchanged a complicated handshake with Luiz. 'See you then, my friend.'

The MC sauntered away down the street. If he was worried that the police were going to catch up with him, he hid it well. Unlike Livio, Luiz knew for certain that no one would be coming after them. He drove slowly around Rio, trying to steel his jangling nerves. Although the morning had gone like clockwork, that had been arranged beforehand. In the *favela*, nothing was planned.

An hour later, he steered his scooter up the steep incline that led towards Santa Marta. As the road narrowed, Luiz felt his heart begin to beat faster. It had been years since he'd last made this journey – but even so, there were certain sights he recognized: shopfronts and cafes, the mission where he and Ana had been taken in before their adoption. Now, however, the walls were plastered with a particular graffiti symbol, spray-painted in black: a cross-shaped gravestone in between the letters C and N. The message was clear. Santa Marta was Comando Negro territory.

Outside a drinks shop, two boys were sitting on the step, warily scanning the street. Lookouts. As Luiz sped past them, one of them frowned and began talking into a radio phone. Unlike other kids, the gangs tended not to use mobiles, wary of their calls being traced. Regardless, it was bad news. After four years away, no one was going to recognize Luiz any more – and strangers didn't try to enter the *favela* alone. Luiz knew that the lookout would be alerting other members of the Comando Negro, the ones standing guard further up the road at the *boca do fumo* – the 'mouth of the smoke'.

Every *favela* boasted at least one *boca*. It served as both a point of sale, where people bought their drugs from the local gangs, and a marker of the entrance to the *favela*. Gangs maintained *bocas* like security checkpoints, with lookouts and armed guards monitoring all the traffic that passed in and out of the *favelas*. Even the police tended not to approach the *bocas* unless they were intent on carrying out a raid. Beyond that point, it was the gangs' law that mattered.

Up ahead, the road banked sharply, creating a narrow

funnel where it curved to the right. There was a building on the corner at the narrowest point, sandbags piled up around its base. A group of boys were milling around the doorway, openly parading their guns. Some were carrying satchels: they would be filled, Luiz knew, with one-gram wraps of cocaine in clear plastic bags.

As he approached, one of the boys stepped forward, levelled his firearm at him and shouted at Luiz to stop. Luiz recognized the weapon from one of Richard Madison's training sessions – an FAL self-loading rifle, powerful enough to punch a sizeable hole through the toughest metal. With a sinking heart, he realized something else as well.

MC Livio was nowhere to be seen.

Luiz slowly brought his scooter to a stop and dismounted.

'Who the hell are you?' spat the boy. 'This *favela* belongs to the Comando Negro. You got a death wish or something?'

'I'm meeting someone here,' Luiz said, trying to keep calm. 'MC Livio – you know him?'

The boy laughed harshly. 'Everyone round here knows Livio. That don't make them his friend. And it sure don't make you mine.'

As a pregnant silence descended, another guard, older than the first, appeared in the doorway of the checkpoint. He stalked over and pushed the other boy in the shoulder.

'Who's this – your new boyfriend?' he said venomously. 'You know that Angel don't want no strangers hanging around the *boca*. Are you going to deal with him or not?'

The mood outside the *boca* was turning ugly. Luiz silently cursed the MC. Was he late or had he just forgotten about him? On the roof of a building beyond the checkpoint, he saw something metallic glinting in the sunlight. More weaponry. Luiz knew that there were firing positions all over the rooftops around the *boca*. It would only take one jumpy finger on the trigger and he would be mowed down in a hail of bullets. He turned around, slowly raising his hands in the air.

'I don't want any trouble,' he said. 'I'm not carrying any guns. Check me if you want.'

Luiz felt the rifle jab him in the back. 'I don't give a shit *what* you're carrying. You'd need an army to get past us. Down on your knees.'

'Just wait for Livio and he'll –'

The other boy smashed the gun against the back of Luiz's legs, sending him sprawling to the floor.

'Wait!' a voice called out.

His heart leaping with relief, Luiz saw MC Livio labouring up the hill towards them, a bulky brown paper bag in his arms.

'He's with me,' the MC called out. 'Don't shoot!'

The gang member swore loudly. 'You cut it pretty fine, Livio,' he shouted back. 'Five more seconds and your friend here would be looking for his brains in the road. What are you doing telling strangers to meet you at the *boca*?'

'I'm here now, aren't I? It's all cool.' Livio pulled Luiz to his feet with a pudgy hand. 'Sorry I'm late, Luiz. Took me longer to sort my shit out than I thought.'

'Just glad you got here when you did.'

'Come on, let's go.'

Nodding at the gang members, Livio moved past the *boca* and into Santa Marta. Luiz took a deep breath and followed him.

8. Santa Marta

Luiz stepped into a riot of colour and noise.

Santa Marta was a warren of alleyways and backstreets that criss-crossed the steep hillside, cutting pathways through rows of rickety, tin-roofed shacks. Many dwellings had been built directly on top of one another, forming precarious tower blocks that looked as though one strong gust of wind could topple them over. They were painted in bright, Day-Glo paint, vibrant shades of pinks and yellows overlaid with Comando Negro graffiti: not just the now-familiar CN gravestone, but vivid murals showing gang members engaged in gun battles with rivals from the Compadres and Quarto Comando. Almost every house seemed to double as a shop, hand-painted signs advertising everything from Cheetos and lollipops to beer and bottled gas. Above Luiz's head, tangled webs of cables conducted illegally tapped electricity back to the houses.

The narrow streets were breathless with activity, young boys kicking footballs around while old women struggled with shopping bags. Shouts of laughter overlapped with scooter horns and blaring TV sets. Somewhere further up the hill, a thumping beat was blasting out from a sound system. Luiz's nostrils were filled with a combustible mixture of diesel, sewage and barbecued meat, while the pungent aroma of marijuana hung thickly in the air. As he looked around the *favela*, memories of his childhood came flooding back and it was hard for Luiz to keep the smile from his face. He realized that, no matter how much time he had spent in the suburbs, a tiny part of him would always be a *favela* boy.

Wherever they went in Santa Marta, everyone they passed in the alleyways seemed to know Livio. Old women called out to him and young girls blew kisses at him. The MC took it in his stride, nodding and smiling at them, his gaze lingering on the prettiest girls. He puffed as he toiled up the steep incline, shifting the brown paper bag in his arms.

'What's in the bag?' Luiz asked curiously.

The MC gave him a long look, then shrugged his shoulders. 'Medicine for my little girl,' he said. 'She's not been so well and it's not easy getting her to a doctor. My wife would have killed me if I hadn't brought it back.'

Luiz glanced at Livio. Though he knew that many of the young boys in the *favelas* had families, the MC was barely a year older than him, and Luiz couldn't begin to imagine taking care of a wife and kids. He was about to ask Livio about his family when the MC gestured for silence.

They had come to the end of a long alleyway and now found themselves in a small, dusty square surrounded on all sides by shacks covered in Comando Negro graffiti.

The joyful energy of the *favela* had disappeared – despite the muggy heat, the atmosphere in the square felt cold.

Livio grabbed Luiz's arm. 'We're here. Leave the talking to me at first, OK? The Comando Negro don't know you and they hate surprises.'

There were only three people in the square, lounging around the entrance to one of the shacks. A boy wearing a bright yellow Brazilian football shirt and orange Ray-Bans was straddling a low wall, music pumping out of a stereo beside him. He drummed the wall in time with the beat. An older boy with bleached-blond hair and a long scar running down his face was slouched on the shack's steps, a bored expression on his face. Slightly removed from his companions, a younger, lighter-skinned boy in a dirty T-shirt was sitting on the ground, scratching at the dusty earth with a stick. Unlike the other two – whose semi-automatic pistols were visible in the waistband of their shorts – he didn't appear to be armed. The boy jumped up excitedly when he saw Livio approaching.

'Hey!' he cried. 'Look who's back!'

'You know it!' Livio greeted him gleefully, slapping his palm in a greeting. 'Can't keep a good man down, Dog.'

'Word was you got arrested,' said Dog, in a high-pitched voice. 'How did you get away?'

'You should have seen it!' Livio replied. 'As soon as we stepped out of the police station some dude started firing at the cops!'

'Who?'

'Who knows? Could have been one of the Comando

Negro, could have been another gang. There's enough people in Rio who want to take a shot at the police, aren't there?'

'It wasn't the Comando Negro,' the boy with the scar said. 'We would have known about it.'

'Whoever it was, I owe them.' Livio laughed.

Dog's eyes widened. 'What happened next, Livio?'

'Shut up, Dog,' the boy with the scar said sharply. 'This is soldiers' business. You wouldn't understand.'

'Yeah, shut it, Dog,' the boy with the Ray-Bans chimed in. 'Or Stripe'll shove that stick of yours up your ass.'

Silenced, Dog looked glumly down at the floor. As Stripe got to his feet and dusted his hands together, Luiz saw that they were trembling slightly. The boy kept brushing his nostrils – a surefire sign that he was on cocaine. 'So what did happen next, Livio?'

'You should have seen it, Stripe. The cops were shitting themselves. We made a break for it when they weren't looking – stole a scooter and drove out.'

'Bullshit,' the boy with the orange Ray-Bans said in a bored voice. 'You've been smoking too much again, Livio.'

'It's true! On my mother's life!'

'Maybe he's telling the truth, Joker,' Stripe said slowly, a slight smile playing on his lips. He sniffed. 'Maybe our man here broke out . . .'

'I tell you, that's what happened!'

'. . . or maybe he did a little deal.'

Stripe's smile suddenly vanished, replaced by a cold, hard stare.

'What are you saying?' asked Livio.

'I'm saying, maybe one of the cops had a word with you, promised to let you go if you did something for them.'

Livio laughed nervously. 'Me, do a deal with the police? Are you nuts?'

'Everyone knows you run with us. Everyone wants to know about the Comando Negro. It makes sense to me.'

'You gotta believe me, Stripe. I never told the cops anything.'

Stripe jerked his head at Luiz, acknowledging him for the first time. 'Who's the stranger?'

Livio put his arm around Luiz's shoulders. 'This is my man Luiz. He got us out. I've never seen anyone who can drive like this guy.'

Stripe stared icily at Luiz.

'And what is he doing here?' the boy said, directing his question at the MC.

Livio spread his arms out. 'Hey, he wanted to see Santa Marta, meet the Comando Negro. You're celebrities, Stripe. Especially since you blew away that basketball player.'

'Angel's not going to like this,' Stripe said softly.

'And you *really* don't want to mess with my bro today,' Joker added, a grin on his face. 'Giselle's been giving him shit again. He's ready to blow.'

A shadow passed across Livio's face. 'Oh. Maybe we should leave it.'

'Why?' Luiz said. 'Who's Angel?'

'Who wants to know?' a voice said behind him.

Luiz whirled round and saw someone standing in the doorway of the shack. Angel was noticeably older than the rest of the group, maybe twenty years of age. He was black, his hair braided into short dreadlocks. An imposing figure, he wore a sleeveless T-shirt that revealed a pair of bulging forearms. In his left hand he carried a sawn-off 12-gauge Remington shotgun, in his right a bottle of Skol beer. Sizing Luiz up, Angel took a swig from the bottle.

'Hey, *dono*,' Stripe began. 'Livio's brought this stranger into the *favela* and –'

'I don't give a shit,' Angel said curtly. 'I gotta meeting to go to.'

'A meeting?' Luiz asked, without thinking.

Angel tossed the beer bottle to one side and strode towards him, moving so close that their faces were nearly touching. Luiz could smell the sweet and sour combination of booze and spliffs on his breath.

'No one said you could talk to me. No one said you could ask me any *questions*!'

'He didn't mean anything by it,' Livio cut in hastily. 'My man Luiz doesn't know the lie of the land round here. He's a good man, though. You should have seen him today at the police station. Drove through gunfire to get us both out.'

'That so?' Angel said, raising an eyebrow. 'And what is he doing here?'

'I wanted to meet the famous Comando Negro,' Luiz replied, glimpsing an opportunity. 'Word is that your cocaine is the best in Rio, and all the other gangs are too chickenshit to take you on. I figure, the size of your operation, maybe you need another driver. For deliveries, stuff like that. Livio can vouch for me – he said it'd be all right for me to come up here.'

'Did he?' whispered the *dono*, in a soft vicious undertone. He jabbed Luiz in the chest. 'I don't care if Livio said you could come here and move in with his mother. He doesn't run Santa Marta – I do. And I don't like strangers with big mouths. If you're not out of the *favela* in the next five minutes, you're a dead man. You hear me?'

Luiz nodded slowly.

'Good. Now piss off.'

Livio placed a chubby hand on Luiz's shoulder. 'Time to go, my friend.' He firmly steered Luiz away from the gang, whispering in his ear, 'Angel always gets like this when Giselle has a go at him. I'll have another word with him later, when he's calmed down.'

'Thanks, man.'

'Shit – it's the least I can do. Thanks to you, I'm going to spend tonight partying instead of sitting in some stinking jail cell. What about you? Where are you going to go?'

'Don't worry about me. I can always find a place to hide out.' Luiz passed Livio a slip of paper with a number on it. 'You can get hold of me here if Angel changes his mind.'

Bidding farewell to the MC, Luiz reluctantly climbed back on his scooter. After the adrenalin rush of the breakout from the police station, the meeting with the Comando Negro had been a massive anticlimax. Now he had to rely on Livio to change Angel's mind – and although he quite liked the MC, Livio wasn't exactly reliable.

Luiz drove slowly back to Trojan's warehouse, wondering how they would react to his return. The guard at the gate recognized him and quickly ushered him inside the compound, calling in on his radio. Before Luiz could park his scooter, Valerie Singer had come out of the warehouse and was crossing the concrete towards him, her hair blowing in the breeze.

'How did it go?'

Luiz grimaced. 'Not great. They told me to piss off. Livio's going to put in a word for me, though. What do we do now?'

Valerie raised an eyebrow. 'Now? We wait, I guess.'

The phone call came late at night.

Submerged in a deep sleep, it took Luiz a while to register the fact that his mobile was ringing. He stretched out a dozy hand and picked up the phone from his bedside table.

'Yeah?' he mumbled.

'Luiz? It's me, Livio.'

Immediately Luiz was awake. The MC's voice was slurred – he sounded like he had been smoking dope all night. There was a thumping bass in the background and the confused sounds of a party.

'Hey, Livio,' Luiz said cautiously. 'What's going on?'

'All kinds of shit, man,' the MC drawled. 'It's madness up here.'

'What's going on?'

'There was a gun battle a few hours ago. Some bastards from the Compadres tried to gatecrash a party here.'

'What happened?'

'Angel happened,' Livio replied meaningfully. 'As soon as he clocked them there was a gun battle. Bullets flying everywhere.'

'Jesus. Did anyone get shot?'

'Don't think so. The Compadres ran for it as soon as they realized they were outnumbered. But the Comando Negro are talking about going to war anyway. It's an honour thing – you can't let shit like that go off on your own turf! And if there's a war, we're going to need more numbers. I've had a word with Angel and he says he'll see you at seven tomorrow evening at the *favela.*'

'That's great!' Luiz said.

'I guess,' Livio slurred back. 'Don't know why you're so eager to get shot at, man. I'm going to go get some pussy before this party ends. See you tomorrow.'

Luiz rang off and put the phone down, his heart thumping. He had done it. He was in.

9. Road Test

As the sun set over Rio, a lone scooter wound its way up the hill towards Santa Marta.

Luiz had spent a long day in Trojan's warehouse, giving exhaustive descriptions of the gang members he had met. No detail was considered too small. After several hours, one of Trojan's technicians had built up startlingly accurate e-fits of the Comando Negro on the computer. Richard Madison was pleased with the results.

'We'll send these over to Oliveira and see if he recognizes any of them,' he said, during a meal of skewered chicken. Sucking his fingers clean of grease, Madison passed Luiz a piece of paper with a number on it.

'What's this?' Luiz asked.

'You can't come back to the warehouse again. It's too dangerous now. You hear anything you think we should know about, call this number and arrange a meeting instead. We don't know who might be listening in, so it's best to talk face to face.'

The Brit noticed the uncertain look on Luiz's face. 'Don't worry. If anyone else uses this number, it'll sound like an ordinary pizza place. But if you ask for a large pizza with black olives, you'll be put straight through to me.'

'Large pizza, black olives,' Luiz repeated. He fingered the gold cross around his neck. 'Is the GPS working OK?'

'You needn't worry about that,' Madison said, laughing. 'You could go deep-sea diving and we'd find you.'

At this rate they might have to, Luiz thought to himself, as he navigated his scooter up the hill. If the Comando Negro discovered his true identity, he'd probably end up at the bottom of the ocean. If he wasn't shot dead or microwaved first.

As the *boca* came into view, Luiz was surprised to see the Comando Negro lined up on the brow of the hill, the sun dying a golden death behind them. Angel stood at the head of the gang, his Remington shotgun resting upright against his shoulder, taking a drag from a fat spliff his brother Joker had handed to him. Stripe and Livio were holding a hushed conference with one another, while Dog skulked unnoticed in the background, his white vest stained with mud.

Angel flicked the remains of the spliff on to the road as Luiz steered his scooter to a stop alongside them, exhaling a cloud of smoke into the air.

'So Livio's been bitching in my ear about how you should be allowed to join the Comando Negro,' said the *dono* finally. 'Even though you're not local, not a Santa Marta boy.'

Luiz spread out his hands. 'I'm still a *carioca* – Rio born and bred. I just don't stay in the same *favela* for too long.

Never know when the heat's going to fall on you, you know?'

'Hear that, boys?' Angel barked. 'We got ourselves a nomad!'

Livio frowned. 'What's a nomad?'

The *dono* shook his head. 'You are one pig-shit ignorant soldier, you know that? It means he doesn't call one place home.' Angel turned back to Luiz. 'And now you want to try your luck in Santa Marta.'

'Just give me a chance,' Luiz replied. 'I'll prove to you I can drive.'

'We'll see about that. Be grateful that the Compadres have decided to try and start a turf war with us. I can't afford to be that choosy about men right now. Here's the deal.'

At a glance from his older brother, Joker tossed Luiz a large package. Through the clear plastic wrapping, he saw that it was filled with white powder.

'Our sister needs this,' Joker said. 'She's got a house over in Flamengo. The cops are always on the lookout for us, so we can't go there.'

'The quickest route is via the highway,' rapped Angel. 'Take it and don't piss about. This is urgent.'

Flamengo was a large residential district of Rio north-east of Botafogo. Following Angel's route, it would only take Luiz half an hour to get there on his bike. He tucked the heavy package under his arm.

'No problem.'

He was about to get on his scooter when Stripe called

him back. The blond-haired boy jerked his head at a black 50cc motorbike leaning against the wall of the *boca*.

'Take my bike.'

'What's wrong with mine?'

'This is the Comando *Negro*, stupid,' sneered Stripe. 'We don't go riding around on white scooters. Take a proper machine.'

Luiz reluctantly walked over to the black motorbike and fired it into life. As he revved the engine, Livio came over with a satchel. 'Best to put the stuff in this, yeah?' he said loudly.

'Cheers, man.'

'Listen up,' Livio whispered suddenly, his voice barely audible above the throaty roar of the bike. 'The highway takes you right through Compadres territory.'

'What!'

'As soon as they see you coming all in black, they're going to start firing. It's a test, Luiz. Angel won't trust you until you prove yourself.'

'Can't I go a different way?'

Livio shook his head. 'There'll be people watching you.'

'But how the hell am I supposed to get past the Compadres?'

'Drive fast?'

'Thanks for that,' Luiz muttered.

Livio smiled. 'I've seen you drive, remember? You'll be fine, man.' The portly MC patted him on the back and stepped away from the bike.

*

As Luiz roared away from the *boca*, Angel watched him, a thoughtful expression on his face. He turned to Joker. 'What do you reckon?'

His brother shrugged. 'If he's as fast as Livio says, maybe he'll make it through alive.'

'Stripe?'

The other boy smiled. 'Dead man walking. Believe me.' He turned and strolled back into the *favela*, whistling a tune to himself.

Luiz began driving in the direction of Flamengo, dark clouds of anger and confusion scudding across his mind. It felt like everyone was out to get him. Trojan Industries had all but blackmailed him to work for them, claiming that they wanted to bring down the gangs – but now, thanks to them, Luiz was couriering cocaine across Rio. The Comando Negro said they'd give him a chance to join their gang, only to send him straight into a trap. Luiz was sorely tempted to throw the packet into a bin, drive back to his parents' house and forget all about this mess. But the image of Ana in the police station wouldn't leave him. His sister was counting on him – he had to do this.

As Luiz rode along the broad, deserted highway, street lights flickered into life above his head. Through the encroaching gloom, he saw a picture of a playing card graffitied on a wall in red spray-paint. It was the King of Diamonds – the tag of the Compadres. He was in enemy territory now. Spying a gang of boys loitering at the side of the highway, Luiz shivered with fearful anticipation. As his black bike zoomed past them, a shout of alarm went up and the evening air was punctured by the crack of a pistol shot.

Luiz sharply twisted the accelerator on the handle, angling the motorbike in a diagonal line away from the Compadres. Risking a quick look back, he saw that two scooters had set off in pursuit. He gunned the 50cc engine again, trying to squeeze every last bit of speed from it. Luiz knew that the Compadres would be contacting one another on their radio phones, word spreading across the *favela* like bushfire. Out here on the highway, he was a sitting duck.

He veered left, heading off down a hill along a narrow road that wound between two rows of shacks. There was another gunshot, then a bullet bit into the road in front of him: a Compadres sniper on the roofs. With no room for manoeuvre, all Luiz could do was bend low over the handlebars and pray that the sniper was unable to get a clear shot at him.

At the bottom of the hill, the way forked. The main part of the road continued to the right, while a dirt track ran off at a sharp angle to the left. Luiz waited until the last second and then threw the motorbike left. The bike skidded on the surface, tipping violently to one side. Clinging on with all his strength, Luiz managed to stay in his seat and sent the bike hurtling down the dirt track.

There was a loud crash behind him. Glancing over his shoulder, Luiz saw the mangled remains of a scooter in the wall at the fork in the road and a boy lying sprawled across the concrete. The other scooter had slowed to negotiate the turn, losing time as it made to follow Luiz.

The dirt track was rough and bumpy; Luiz had to swerve to avoid a pair of chickens scratching around in the dirt. The *favela* was busier here, throbbing to the sound of music and the chatter of the locals as they sat outside their houses in the warm evening. Luiz ploughed on, disregarding the shouts of protest from the onlookers.

Figures were scrambling in the gloom further along the track, dragging large crates into his path. The Compadres were setting up a roadblock. Luiz dived into a side alley, sending the motorbike juddering down a flight of steps. He drove blindly through the darkness, relying on instinct to negotiate a way. With a bump the bike righted itself, as the steps came out on to a mercifully flat passage. At the end of the alley, Luiz recognized the welcoming lights of Rua Pinheiro Machado, the main road that marked the beginning of the Flamengo district. If he could just make it there, he would be safe.

The engine coughed violently beneath him and the motorbike slowed to a crawl. He had run out of petrol.

'Shit!'

Luiz scrambled off the bike and furiously hurled it to one side. That was why Stripe had made him take it. He wasn't supposed to get out of the Compadres territory alive.

The dire whine of scooter engines was getting louder in his ears. His pursuers were closing in. He had to move. Holding on to the satchel tightly, Luiz tumbled over a wall and began running round the back of a row of shacks. Meanwhile, in the alleyway, he could hear the Compadres shouting and swearing at one another as they discovered his bike.

'Spread out!' one of them called. 'That Negro bastard can't have got far.'

Luiz rounded the corner of a shack at pace, only to crash headlong into someone. Startled, he saw a boy his age dressed all in red, a pistol in his hand. Luiz had run straight into a Compadre.

The boy looked at him in amazement, too surprised to raise his gun. Luiz didn't hesitate, dropping down and sweeping the Compadre's legs out from under him. As the boy made to shout, Luiz drove a knee into his stomach, knocking the air from his lungs. The Compadre curled up in pain, allowing Luiz to wrestle the boy's weapon away from him. He flicked off the safety catch and took aim.

The boy looked up, tears welling in his eyes, to see a gun barrel pointing at him.

'Please . . .' he whimpered.

Luiz broke away, took aim again, then stopped. With an oath, he hurled the pistol into a nearby bush and sprinted away from the boy. Hurdling a low wire fence, he dropped on to Rua Pinheiro Machado and began running into Flamengo. He had escaped.

Twenty minutes later, Luiz found himself jogging down the road where Angel's sister lived. Compared to Santa Marta, this neighbourhood was a suburban haven of detached houses and neat lawns. After his encounter with the Compadres, the quiet seemed deafening in Luiz's ears.

He stopped at a small house at the end of the street. Through the glass door, he saw Angel's sister was waiting for him, cradling a wailing baby in her arms. She barely looked up at him as he entered the house.

'You're late,' she said.

'Nearly didn't make it at all.'

The girl placed the baby carefully down in a cot, making soft soothing sounds. Looking at her closely, Luiz thought she was a little bit older than him – eighteen or so. As her baby quietened, she turned briskly to Luiz.

'You got the stuff?'

Luiz nodded and handed her the package. She gave it a critical glance, then took it into the kitchen, tore open the plastic and – to Luiz's amazement – calmly began tipping the white powder down the sink.

'What are you doing?' Luiz gasped. 'I nearly died bringing you that! It's gotta be worth a fortune!'

'Depends how much you want clean clothes,' the girl replied, scraping the last of the white crystals from the bag. 'It's washing powder.'

'What?'

'It's not like I could tell what brand, but it sure isn't cocaine.'

'I nearly got shot . . . for washing powder?' Luiz muttered in disbelief.

'Hey, it's not like you *had* to drive through Compadres territory either. It was a test, wasn't it? And my brother

81

isn't called Joker for nothing.' Noticing the dumbfounded look on his face, she punched Luiz playfully on the arm. 'Cheer up. You made it, didn't you? You're a member of the Comando Negro!'

Luiz nodded dumbly, slumping against the sideboard. The girl tossed the torn packet into a bin.

'Now it gets *really* dangerous,' she said, and laughed.

10. Dog Sitting

Unwilling to take any more risks that evening, Luiz caught a bus back through town, steering well clear of Compadres territory. By the time he had returned to Santa Marta, it was the middle of the night. Word must have got through that Luiz had passed the test, because the guards at the *boca* waved him in. There was no one he knew waiting for him, though, and he didn't have a clue where he was supposed to go.

Reaching the main street on Santa Marta, Luiz saw that things were just beginning to warm up. People were sitting outside in the night-time heat, chatting and joking with one another. *Baile funk* poured out of every speaker, the different beats overlapping with one another, creating a barrage of noise. Luiz had to step out of the way of taxi scooters as they barrelled down the street, beeping their horns.

A familiar figure was sitting at a table outside a cafe, a Skol in one hand and a bulky spliff in the other. As he saw Luiz approaching, MC Livio grinned and got up.

'You lucky bastard,' he chuckled, enveloping Luiz in a bear hug and clapping him on the back. 'Everyone's talking about how you made it past the Compadres. You and that bike!'

'No thanks to Stripe,' Luiz muttered.

The MC was too stoned to pick up on Luiz's meaning. Instead, he gestured vaguely at the group of people sitting around the table.

'We're just getting started here. Sit down and let's celebrate.'

Luiz shook his head. 'I'm shattered. You know anywhere I can crash for the night?'

Livio stubbed out his spliff in the ashtray.

'I can do better than that,' he said. 'I'll show you.'

Bidding farewell to the rest of the table, Livio led him away from the bustling main road. They walked through a dark maze of alleyways and dirt tracks, and it wasn't long before Luiz was completely lost. Although the *favela* was quieter here, the music never completely abandoned them.

Livio finally stopped outside a shack with a battered, corrugated-iron roof and pushed open the door.

'You can stay at my place for a while,' he said.

Following the MC inside, Luiz found himself in a small front room, sparsely lit by a lone light bulb. There was little in the way of furniture – a couple of chairs, a gas stove and a stereo. An old mattress was spread out on the floor.

'For when I have guests,' Livio explained, his nudge informing Luiz that those guests would be almost certainly female.

'Where's your family?'

'Gabriela lives in her place across the *favela* with the kids. I come here when I want to relax. Can't do that with kids running around and Gabriela nagging me. You know what women are like.'

Livio flicked on the strip light in the kitchen and produced two large bottles of Skol from the fridge. Luiz accepted his gratefully and took a deep swig. It was only now that he realized how thirsty he was.

Plumping down in the chairs, they talked for hours, drinking beer and listening to music. After all that had happened in the past few days, it felt unreal to be doing something normal. The more time he spent with the chubby MC, the more Luiz liked him. Compared to the rest of the Comando Negro, he was relaxed, even friendly. The MC smoked spliffs for the entire night, his eyes becoming more glazed and his speech less distinct.

Even though Luiz was still on his guard, he needed to unwind. He didn't usually drink alcohol, so it didn't take long for him to feel drunk. After a couple of bottles, he looked thoughtfully at Livio.

'You're not like the rest of them, are you?'

'Who?'

'The Comando Negro.'

Livio shrugged. 'This is the *favela*, my friend. We're all in it together. We laugh together, fight together, bleed together.'

'Die together?'

'Probably. How many old people d'you see walking around here? Soldiers like us don't live very long. Angel's made it to twenty, but he's the toughest I ever saw. How long d'you think Dog's got? Shit, Luiz, he won't make it past twelve! I'm just glad I've made it this far.'

'What about your music? Wouldn't you rather do that instead?'

'I love music, but this . . .' Livio frowned, trying to think of the words. 'This is *life*, man. This is what it is.' He sparked up another spliff and took a long drag on it, the end burning brightly in the dingy light.

Luiz woke up on the floor, an empty bottle by his side. MC Livio was standing over him, poking him in the ribs with his foot.

'Wake up, you lazy bastard!' he shouted. 'Time to go!'

'Ow! Stop yelling!' Luiz groaned. 'Go where?'

'It's delivery day.'

'What's that?'

'You'll see. Come on. Get ready.'

Luiz washed quickly in a basin and headed outside, wincing in the bright sunshine. Angel was waiting for him, flanked by the rest of the Comando Negro command.

'Looks like you made it in,' he said.

'Just about,' Luiz said flatly. He turned to Stripe. 'You know the bike you made me ride? The petrol ran out.'

'Yeah?' Stripe looked as though he couldn't care less. 'Thought it had a full tank. Sorry about that, Luiz.'

Angel beckoned to Livio. 'Come on, MC. Time to go.'

Luiz made to follow, only for the *dono* to put a hand against his chest. 'Where the hell d'you think you're going?'

'Delivery day?'

'You must be kidding me. You may be able to ride a motorbike, but you aren't a *soldado* yet. Leave the men to take care of delivery day. You stay here with Dog at the *boca*.'

'I've got to stay here?'

'Hope you can change nappies!' Joker sniggered.

'Hey – take me with you! I passed your initiation, didn't I? I'm Comando Negro, I can –'

Luiz didn't even see the punch. There was a sudden movement and he was on the floor, the taste of blood in his mouth. His head spinning, Luiz looked up to see Angel standing over him.

'Listen to me. If Livio hadn't spoken for you, I'd have shot you when you first walked in here. I got respect for Livio – everyone round here does. But if you want respect, you're going to have to earn it.' Angel dropped to his haunches and grabbed Luiz's hair, jerking his head back. 'Get in my face again and I'll kill you.'

He stood up again, flicking blood from his hand. 'Now stay here with Dog and try not to mess anything up.'

Angel stalked away, Joker following hot on his heels. As Luiz rolled groggily into a sitting position, he saw Livio casting a grave look in his direction before he too walked away. Stripe was the last to leave. The blond-haired boy snorted with laughter and flicked a cigarette butt at Luiz's feet, contempt burning in his eyes.

'You should have stayed in that cell with Livio,' he said. 'Kids with big mouths don't last long here.'

Several hours later and Luiz and Dog were sitting on top of a wall by the Santa Marta *boca do fumo*, their legs dangling

87

over the edge. From their vantage point, they could see a heat haze shimmering above the Rio skyline. Armies of coloured paper kites were arcing through the sky, battling for supremacy in the wind.

Further down from them, two younger boys from the Comando Negro were also perched on the wall, balancing satchels on their knees. They had spent the day doling out wraps of cocaine to a steady stream of customers. In his time away from the *favela*, Luiz had forgotten the sheer range of people who bought drugs from the *boca*. It wasn't just twitching addicts sidling up for a fix, but people from all different parts of Rio society: from middle-class suburban kids who crept up nervously, their eyes darting this way and that, to the elderly cleaning women on their way home from the hotels in Zona Sul, who bought the drugs as casually as they did the rest of their shopping.

Although his nose had stopped bleeding, Luiz's face was still sore from Angel's punch. Luiz was still cursing himself for being so foolish. He was going to have to be extra careful around the *dono* of the Comando Negro from now on. Dog, however, was a different matter. He wasn't a bad kid, Luiz thought. Maybe that was the problem. He was too eager to please, too eager to impress. For all his swagger, it was obvious he didn't have what it took to be a soldier. He was never going to be able to pull the trigger.

Dog pointed up into the sky. 'You see the kites? Few months back, I would have been flying one of those. Before I got promoted.'

'Yeah?'

'They're signals,' Dog said, pleased by the opportunity to show off his knowledge. 'Different coloured kites mean different things. Like, if you see a red kite flying, you know there's trouble on the way. A rival gang or the cops.'

The little boy nudged Luiz. 'We used to stick glass to the strings, try and cut through the other lines. One afternoon, I brought down three other kites. The other kids were so pissed off!'

'Really?' Luiz said. Though he remembered the kite signals from his own time in Santa Marta, he acted as though this was new information. He feigned an innocent look. 'You must know a lot about the Comando Negro, being around Angel all the time.'

'I hear it all, Luiz,' Dog boasted. 'No one pays any attention to me, but I'm always listening.'

'How come you didn't go with everyone else to the delivery?'

'They won't let me. It's all Stripe's fault.' Dog's face darkened. 'I hate Stripe. He's always picking on me, saying I'm never going to be a *soldado*. He thinks everyone's scared of him – one day I'm going to show him.'

'Where does the delivery happen?'

'They won't tell me. Some warehouse downtown. The trucks carrying all the shit come in from Colombia and they don't go into the *favela*. I wish I could see it.'

Luiz nudged him. 'Someone's got to protect the *favela* while they're away. Big responsibility, that.'

'Yeah.' Dog smiled, puffing his chest out. 'Everything's OK when I'm in charge. Not like when Angel goes to meet the Doctor. Then Stripe's in charge and all he does is push me around.'

'The Doctor?' Luiz asked quickly. 'Who's that?'

Dog fell silent, a pensive look on his face. 'I'm not supposed to talk about him.'

'You can talk to me, Dog. Hey, I'm Comando Negro too!'

The little boy glanced left and right, then whispered, 'He's the money man. Angel's just the muscle; it's the Doctor who brings in the drugs. He only deals with Angel – no one else has even seen him. That's all I can tell you.'

'It's not very much.'

'It's not that I don't trust you, Luiz, but Angel gets angry when –'

Dog broke off as Luiz grabbed his arm.

A lone red kite was fluttering in the breeze.

Luiz stood up on the wall and looked down the hill, shielding his eyes from the sun. To his amazement, he saw a tidal wave of people sweeping up towards the *favela*.

'What's going on?'

'Must be a police raid,' Dog replied. 'They're coming to get a hit before the cops show up.' He scrambled to his feet. 'Let's get out of here.'

'Aren't we supposed to stay and protect the *boca*?'

Dog laughed incredulously. 'Take on the police? Without Angel? You must be crazy! Look, everyone's getting out of here.'

Further along the wall, a desperate crowd had gathered beneath the two Comando Negro members selling the cocaine. Ignoring the pleas and waving banknotes, the two boys gathered up their satchels and scampered past Luiz after the rapidly retreating figure of Dog. Down below them, Luiz could now see two black police vans hurtling up the hillside towards the *boca*. Dog was right – they were going to be badly outnumbered if they stayed here. He turned and sprinted across the rooftops after the rest of the Comando Negro, feeling a small surge of triumph as he did so. His conversation with Dog had provided him with the first few pieces of information he could pass on to Trojan.

When they were safely back in the depths of the *favela*, Luiz left Dog trying to boss around some younger boys and slipped away down a deserted alleyway. Checking to see that there was no one else around, he took out his mobile phone – which he had smuggled into the *favela* in his sock – and tapped in the number Richard Madison had given him.

The phone rang a couple of times and then a voice on the other end answered. 'Ricardo's Pizzeria.'

'Hi. Can I get a large pizza with black olives?'

After a pause the man said, 'Hold the line.'

There was a click and then Luiz heard Richard Madison's British accent. 'What is it, Luiz?'

'I need a meeting.'

'OK. Can you get away tomorrow night?'

'I guess so.'

'South side of Engenhão stadium, then. Eight o'clock.'

11. Grudge Match

Engenhão stadium rose out of the gloom like a giant spaceship, the white arched girders that towered above the arena gleaming in the floodlights. Some reckoned Botafogo's recently built home ground to be the most modern in all of South America. Pity about the team that played in it, the locals grumbled to one another.

Twenty minutes before the game was due to kick off and the Botafogo fans were streaming towards the stadium in a riot of flags and whirling scarves. It seemed as though everyone was dressed in black-and-white stripes, the colours of the home team. The air rang with chanting and clapping.

Luiz walked quickly through the manic carnival, his head down and his hands thrust into the pockets of his hoodie. Paranoia haunted his every step. His eyes darting this way and that, he was convinced that at any moment he would catch sight of Angel, Stripe or MC Livio. It seemed ridiculous to say, but Luiz was almost more nervous outside the *favela* than inside it. If any of the Comando Negro had decided to go to the Botafogo game and saw Luiz talking with a stranger from outside Santa Marta, that was it. No questions asked. The next time he set foot in the *favela*, he was a dead man.

At the south side of the stadium, Luiz slipped away from the main throng of fans, furtively searching for a familiar face. To his surprise, he caught sight of the broad-shouldered figure of Darius Jordan leaning against a concrete pillar, calmly flicking through a copy of *O Globo*. The head of Trojan Industries was dressed in knee-length shorts and a Botafogo football shirt – just another fan waiting for the game to begin.

He looked up sharply from his newspaper as Luiz approached. 'What happened to your face?'

'The Comando Negro happened to my face,' Luiz replied sourly.

'I see. Let's get inside, shall we?'

He folded his newspaper, slipped it under one arm and led Luiz through the turnstiles into the ground. They went up a flight of stone steps and came out on to the south stand, blinking in the glare of the floodlights. Jordan made his way to a pair of bright blue seats at the top of the stand, which afforded a sweeping view of the pitch. Even though the stadium was barely half full, the cacophonous chanting carried across the night sky.

Luiz had barely taken his seat before the two teams filed out on to the pitch, greeted by a primeval roar. Red flares exploded into life among the crowd on the opposite side of the stadium. A lifelong Botafogo fan, Luiz couldn't help standing up and joining in with the cheers.

Jordan eyed him with amusement. 'Soccer fans,' he said,

with a shake of the head. 'I'll never understand why you love this game so much.'

Expecting Jordan to unleash a barrage of questions, Luiz was surprised when the head of Trojan seemed content merely to watch the game. They sat in silence for much of the first half as Botafogo raced into a two-goal lead, their quicksilver centre forward bagging a brace.

It wasn't until the second half, as the fans around them revelled in their lead, that Jordan settled back in his seat and said, 'So, you want to tell me how things are going?'

Luiz shrugged, his eyes remaining fixed on the game. 'I'm still alive.'

'So I see. They're beginning to trust you?'

'They don't trust anyone. Especially people they've just met.'

'What have you learned?'

'Yesterday was delivery day. A shipment of drugs was being delivered somewhere downtown. I tried to go with the Comando Negro to see where, but they wouldn't let me. I had to stay in the *favela*.'

Jordan nodded. 'Yes, that would make sense. We suspect that the Comando Negro are receiving cocaine shipments via trucks coming over the Colombian border. They can't just drive straight into Santa Marta, so the drugs are stored somewhere downtown and shipped in smaller quantities up to the *favela*. Once it's safely arrived, the gang cuts up the cocaine, mixes it with chalk powder or bicarbonate of soda to make it more profitable, then sells it in the *favelas* in one-gram packages. Not that your average member of the Comando Negro sees much of the profits.' He paused. 'Anything else?'

'This kid Dog mentioned some guy called the Doctor. Said he's the main man, not Angel. Apparently he's the one who's buying the drugs.'

Jordan glanced at him sharply. 'The Doctor? No first name? No other clues?'

Luiz shook his head. 'Dog says he only talks to Angel. No one else has even seen him. Seeing how jumpy Dog got just talking about them makes me think the guy's probably another psycho.'

'Don't make too many assumptions,' said Jordan. 'If this Doctor is the money man, he could be very different from your typical *favela* gang member. He needs some sort of cover to get the shipments in from Colombia. Maybe he's a legitimate businessman, someone with a good reason to have trucks going back and forth across the border.' The American frowned. 'But if Angel is the only contact the Doctor has with the Comando Negro we may have a problem. I showed your descriptions of the gang to Juan Oliveira and he recognized your man Angel right away. His real name is Wilson Rodriguez. Until the Comando Negro set up, he ran with the Compadres.'

'What? But he was fighting the Compadres the other night!'

'He's going to be fighting them for the rest of his life. You don't just switch gangs, Luiz. On the other hand, Angel can take care of himself. He's famous for that shotgun of his for a reason. Oliveira can't even begin to guess how many people he's killed. You're going to have to be incredibly careful around him. This guy shoots first and asks questions later. Getting close enough to him isn't going to be a walk in the park.'

Luiz gave Jordan a sideways glance. 'No shit. I'm just waiting for him to stop punching me in the face so I can ask him a few questions.'

The American refused to rise to the bait. 'If you think that'll work,' he said calmly. 'You know what we need, Luiz. It's up to you how you get it.'

'That's easy for you to say,' Luiz grumbled. 'You don't know what it's like up there!'

Darius raised an eyebrow. 'You think I don't know what gang life is like, son? Shit, Luiz, I wrote the book on it.'

An angry roar went up from the crowd around them. The referee was brandishing a yellow card at one of the Botafogo players, who pressed his palms together in a prayer of innocence.

'You were in a gang?' Luiz asked.

'A long time ago,' Darius said, nodding. 'Back in Detroit.'

'But Richard Madison said you were in the special forces!'

'Well, for that I have to thank Judge Clarence Hopkins,' Darius said. He chuckled at Luiz's puzzled expression. 'When I was eighteen, I found myself in Judge Hopkins's courtroom, charged with a variety of automobile offences. I'm sure a car enthusiast like yourself knows how it is. Anyway, the judge gave me a choice: jail or the army.'

'And you went into the army?'

'Jail didn't sound like my sort of place – though for the first couple of years in the army, I found myself wishing I was in a nice cosy cell. But eventually I adapted, got to like the military way of life – got good at it too. After a few years I was selected for Delta Force and spent ten years on counterterrorist missions all around the world: Grenada, Panama, Iraq – and some other places we don't talk about so much. By the time I got out, I was a very different person from the eighteen-year-old boy in that courtroom. I had discipline, drive. I went into business and made a good deal of money. Carved out the sort of life a man can take pride from. Over thirty years later, I still remember the name Clarence Hopkins, and I still thank him for where he got me.'

Luiz frowned. 'Is that why you started Trojan – because you were in a gang?'

There was a long pause before Darius replied.

'Guilt's a different sort of enemy from the one I was used to. I couldn't hide from it. Couldn't kill it. I tried to pay it off for a while – wrote out cheque after cheque back in Detroit for *this* special programme, *that* charitable foundation. But no matter how much money I spent, I was still turning on the TV and seeing young people killing one another, while governments sat back and washed their hands of it. So I decided to do something a little more proactive – contacted a few old friends from special ops and put Trojan together. Which is how we find ourselves where we are today.'

Luiz shook his head incredulously. 'This is crazy. You're doing all this because you hotwired a couple of cars thirty years ago?'

'I did a lot more than steal automobiles, Luiz,' Darius said grimly. 'Sometimes you just don't get caught. Believe me when I say that, had I been, I wouldn't have been given the army option. At best, I'd still be in prison now.'

Looking into his boss's eyes, Luiz felt a cold chill run down his spine. 'What did you do?'

If Darius Jordan replied, his answer was drowned out by a jubilant cheer from the crowd. All around them people were clapping and bouncing up and down, waving their scarves above their heads. Luiz looked down through the melee, to see the ball nestling in the opposition net and the Botafogo players celebrating in a huddle down by the corner flag. Jordan wasn't looking at the pitch, but gazing off into the middle distance.

'Mr Jordan?'

Disturbed from his reverie, Jordan clapped Luiz on the shoulder. 'Let's get out of here,' he said. 'I've seen enough.'

They got up from their seats and walked down and out of the ground. With twenty minutes of the game remaining, the concrete plaza outside the stadium was quiet. Luiz could still hear the echoes of the crowd roaring and shouting from within Engenhão. Jordan stopped beneath a street lamp, nodding his head in the opposite direction to Santa Marta.

'I'm going this way. Remember what I said about Angel.

Take care around him. You hear anything about the Doctor, anything at all, you contact us, OK? He's the key to this now. We find out his identity, we can bring down the Comando Negro.'

'What about Ana?' Luiz asked suddenly. 'Is she OK? I want to see her.'

Jordan nodded. 'I'll see what I can arrange. Try not to worry about her. As long as we're looking after her, she's safe. Right now, you're the one in danger.'

'Tell me about it,' Luiz replied.

Pulling up his hood, he slipped his hands back into the pockets of his hoodie. He could feel Jordan watching him as he turned to walk away.

'Luiz?'

He looked back at the head of Trojan.

'You're doing well, son. Keep it up.'

Luiz was about to make a sarcastic reply, but bit it back when he saw the look on Darius Jordan's face in the light of the street lamp. Instead he nodded and melted away into the night.

12. Game Over

'Goooooaaaaaaaaalllllllllll!'

Joker's voice echoed around the pitch as he wheeled away in triumph, arms outstretched like an aeroplane's wings. As his teammates rushed to join in the celebrations, the opposition threw up their arms in frustration, pointing fingers of blame at one another. The goalkeeper went trudging after the ball, abuse ringing in his ears.

The pitch was towards the summit of the Santa Marta hillside, a dusty playing surface separating two sets of goalposts, their white paint peeling in the sunlight. With Angel away at another meeting with the Doctor and the *boca* quiet for once, a battered football had been produced and a quick game organized. It was the happiest Luiz had been since he had re-entered Santa Marta. On the pitch he was able to forget about Trojan Industries and black ops, drug deals and the Comando Negro. There were only his teammates and the opposition.

However, what had started as a jokey kick-around was rapidly developing into something rather more serious. Luiz blamed the girls. Before they had turned up, everyone had been messing about, trying to outdo one another with extravagant tricks and ball-juggling. But when a group of pretty girls had gathered at the side of the pitch to watch, the atmosphere had tightened a notch. Nobody wanted to look stupid in front of them. Suddenly the tackles went in harder than before and no one on the pitch was laughing.

All apart from Joker, that is. Angel's brother seemed incapable of taking anything seriously. Even now, as the ball looped up into the air towards him, he stooped over and nonchalantly trapped the ball on the back of his neck. Flicking the ball up again, he volleyed it back to his keeper – the diminutive figure of Dog, looking tiny between the goalposts.

'Robinho can suck my dick,' Joker cackled, grabbing his crotch. 'I'm the best footballer in Brazil.'

For all his showboating, Luiz was glad Joker was on his team. According to Livio, Joker was the best player in the *favela* – good enough to have had trials with one of Rio's youth teams, if he could have been bothered to turn up. And even on the rough, uneven surface, it was easy to see why: Joker was a slick con artist, seemingly presenting the ball to the opposition before a last-second flick or a drag-back took the ball away. His dummies invited lunging challenges, only for a sudden change of direction that left his opponents sliding in the dirt.

Given the sudden change in atmosphere, Luiz was grateful that he too was a decent player. As Joker rolled the ball towards him, he let it run through his legs and spun away from his marker, earning appreciative shouts from his side. After laying off the ball to a teammate, Luiz noticed a small brunette wearing a pink halter top smiling at him shyly from the sidelines. She blushed as Luiz grinned at her, her friends bursting into giggles.

MC Livio jogged up to Luiz, his football shirt dark with sweat stains, and nudged him in the ribs. 'Looks like you've got a fan there.'

'Maybe.'

'Well, you can play with Marie later. For now, keep your mind on the game. It's all square and I'm not losing to these pretty boys.'

Livio jogged off again, waving his arms and calling for the ball. Luiz had to admit, he had been amazed by how at ease the roly-poly MC was on the pitch. Despite his size, Livio had fast feet and a surprisingly nimble touch. He was right too: given the amount of good players on their side, Luiz's team should have been winning comfortably. The fact that they weren't was down to one reason alone: Stripe.

Ruthless and efficient with a gun in his hand, with the ball at his feet it was a different matter for the Comando Negro's chief soldier. He stumbled around the pitch, his clumsy touches sending the ball spinning out of his control. Unwilling to accept the fact that he might be at fault, Stripe raged at his teammates for supposedly poor passes or lack of support. Were it not for the furious expression on his face, it would have been funny.

With the ball at his feet, Joker checked his watch and shouted, 'Next goal's the winner!'

He knocked the ball smoothly to Livio, who held the ball up before returning the pass. With the move building up on the other side of the pitch, Luiz slipped past his marker and made for the right-hand corner of the penalty area. Spotting his movement in one glance, Joker stroked an inch-perfect ball beyond the defence and into his path.

As Luiz bore down on the goal, the opposition keeper came racing from between the posts to narrow the angle. Luiz shaped to shoot, only to step over the ball and knock it towards the byline. Caught off balance, the keeper crashed into Luiz, but not before Luiz had squeezed the ball across the face of the empty net, where Stripe was charging in to smash it home. As Luiz went tumbling to the ground, he looked up, expecting to see the winning goal flying between the posts.

Instead, he watched in disbelief as Stripe screwed the ball wide.

For a few seconds there was a shocked silence. Then Joker threw his head back and roared with laughter, clutching at his sides.

'I don't believe it!' he cried, pointing at Stripe. 'You missed an empty net! Man, you suck!'

Stripe whirled round and glared at Joker.

'Are you blind?' he shouted back. 'The ball bobbled up! Lousy pitch!'

He kicked the goalpost so hard it shivered. As Joker continued to point and laugh, Luiz saw a look of concern cross Livio's face. Stripe didn't have a sense of humour at the best of times and he was being humiliated in public here.

'Cut it out, Joker,' the MC called out. 'The ball *did* bobble – I saw it.'

The boy ignored him. 'Don't worry, Stripe. Football's not your game, that's all. Why don't we stop and play netball instead?'

No one else would have dared to mock Stripe in this way. But then, Joker was Angel's kid brother. Touch him and the *dono* of the Comando Negro would come after you with his shotgun. Not even Stripe was crazy enough to take Angel on.

The opposition had stopped playing and were milling around nervously.

On the other side of the pitch, Dog clapped his hands together. 'Why have we stopped playing? Next goal the winner!'

Stripe paused, then broke away from the group and stalked towards his goalkeeper, ignoring Livio's attempts to call him back. As Stripe closed in on him, Dog waved his hands in the air.

'Hey, Stripe, come on! What are you doing?'

Saying nothing, Stripe walked right up to Dog and head-butted him in the face. The younger boy squealed with pain, clutching his nose as he collapsed to the floor. Following up, Stripe kicked Dog viciously in the ribs. There were horrified murmurs from the crowd; one of the girls buried her face in her friend's shoulder and started to cry.

'We'll start playing when I say so!' Stripe bellowed. 'You hear me, you little shit?'

They cast two dark silhouettes against the blazing

sunlight: one lying on the floor, the other standing threat-eningly over him. Luiz watched in horror as Stripe reached down to his sock, pulled a miniature .22 pistol free from its strapping and took deliberate aim at Dog's head.

'Hey!' Luiz cried out. 'Leave him alone!'

Racing over to Stripe, he grabbed hold of his left arm and pulled him away. For a second a look of astonishment passed across Stripe's face, as though he couldn't believe anyone would dare to stop him. Then he spun around and pointed the .22 at Luiz, his hand shaking with rage.

'You don't get to tell me anything,' the boy spat. 'Joker's got Angel to protect him. That fat MC has got friends all over the *favela*. Even this little shit Dog probably isn't worth the bullet. But you, Luiz? I don't care what anyone says – you aren't Comando Negro. I wouldn't think twice about putting a bullet right *here*.' Stripe pressed his index finger between Luiz's eyes. 'In fact, I'd enjoy it.'

'It's just a game of football, Stripe,' Luiz said softly.

Stripe looked around at the crowd watching him.

'Forget it,' he muttered, stuffing the miniature pistol into his shorts' pocket. 'Game's over.'

He stomped off the pitch, barging his way through the group of girls. The pitch had plunged into silence. Though everyone in Santa Marta had witnessed violence at one time or another, the suddenness of Stripe's explosion had still been shocking. Even Joker looked taken aback.

Luiz crouched by Dog, patting him on the shoulder as the little boy sobbed uncontrollably, his face drenched with blood and his nose twisted out of shape.

Livio walked towards them, shaking his head.

'Pretty brave, getting involved like that,' the MC said. 'Stripe's not going to forget, you know.'

'I know,' Luiz nodded, watching Stripe disappear into the *favela*. 'Neither am I.'

13. Room Service

An uncomfortable silence hung over Santa Marta.

Luiz was sitting in the small *favela* square outside Angel's shack with the leaders of the Comando Negro, the sunlight beating down on the back of his neck. Livio had disappeared off on a mysterious errand and Dog had been in hiding since the football game, presumably licking his wounds. That left Luiz with only Angel, Joker and Stripe for company – and he didn't feel comfortable with any of them. The two brothers spoke to one another in low murmurs, while Stripe ignored Luiz, wrapped up in checking his new gun: a chrome-plated AK-47 assault rifle. The blond-haired boy had stopped speaking to Luiz altogether, apparently content with shooting him the occasional murderous glance.

Luiz was relieved when the quiet was finally broken by a beeping horn. A battered Chevrolet rounded the corner and pulled into the square. Through the dirty windscreen, Luiz saw that Livio was in the front seat, his tongue poking out with concentration as he peered over the steering wheel.

'What's going on?' asked Luiz, as the car rolled to a stop in a cloud of dust.

It was Angel who replied. 'The Doctor's set up a deal in the Zona Sul. We need wheels.'

'You're dealing outside Santa Marta?' said Luiz in surprise. 'Bit risky, isn't it?'

'It's worth it,' replied Angel. 'Some big-shot businessman staying in the Hotel Real wants to buy a load of blow. It's going to make us a fortune.'

Stripe shrugged, brushing his fingers across his nostrils. 'Inside the *favela*, outside the *favela* – who gives a shit? We're Comando Negro. If anyone gets in our way, we open fire.'

Joker circled Livio's car, kicking the tyres suspiciously. 'This is a real shitheap, Livio. Why couldn't you have got something classy like a Porsche or a Ferrari? I can't have no women seeing me driving around in this!'

'It was the best I could do!' Livio protested, as he climbed out of the car. 'Angel asked me to get a car – I got him a car. No one said anything about Porsches and Ferraris!'

'With good reason,' Angel said. 'No one's going to look twice at us in that. Cops see us driving round the Zona Sul in a Porsche, they're going to pull us over.' He cuffed his brother around the back of the head. 'You need to stop thinking with your dick all the time, Rafael. This is serious.'

It was the first time Luiz had heard anyone call Joker by his real name. Although the *dono* had said it softly, his brother's face fell and he went silent. The mood in the square had changed as suddenly as the current at Ipanema Beach – when the Comando Negro prepared for action, the wisecracks stopped. Watching the gang calmly loading their guns, Luiz was reminded who he was dealing with. They were drug dealers and killers – even Livio, who was hauling two suitcases filled with cocaine into the boot of the car.

Mindful of his last run-in with Angel, Luiz stood in the background and kept his mouth shut. He was surprised, therefore, when the *dono* sought him out and came over to speak to him.

'Heard you stepped in with Stripe the other day,' he said. 'Takes a lot of balls to do that.'

'Someone had to do something,' replied Luiz. 'He was going to kill Dog.'

Angel scrutinized him closely, his brown eyes betraying a fierce intelligence. Despite his fearsome reputation as a killer, the *dono* wasn't all muscle. Eventually Angel nodded, as though he had made up his mind about something.

'Get in,' he said, jerking his head towards the car.

'You want me to come with you?' Luiz asked, surprised.

'Think I'm going to let Livio drive? I haven't got a death wish, asshole.'

Angel barked with laughter – the first time Luiz had heard that sound from him – and punched him on the shoulder. The *dono* took up residence in the front passenger seat, while Joker, Livio and Stripe squeezed into the back.

Luiz settled in behind the wheel and turned on the engine. The car started with an arthritic splutter. As he steered the car through the winding roads of the *favela*, Luiz saw that Joker was right about one thing – the car was a bomb. Gears scraped agonizingly as he changed them, while the engine's every hacking cough sounded as though it could be the last. All this, and they were going downhill. The car might be able to make it to the hotel, but whether it could get them home again afterwards was another matter entirely. It took all of Luiz's skill behind the wheel to get them out of Santa Marta and into the early-afternoon traffic of the Zona Sul.

The Hotel Real took pride of place on Avenida Atlantica, the long road that arced around the back of Copacabana Beach. It was a grand, imposing building with a white stucco front, granting those rich enough to afford the best rooms a sweeping view of the Atlantic Ocean. The most famous hotel in Rio, for decades the Real had been the choice of actors, rock stars and the jet-set elite.

Now, as Luiz nursed the ailing car towards the building, he saw two women in crisp tennis whites striding towards the entrance, their long legs luxuriously tanned.

Livio giggled.

'Angel, how the hell are we supposed to blend in here? We take one step in there and they'll call the cops.'

'That's why we're going round the back, dickhead. Keep driving, Luiz, and take a first right after the hotel.'

Angel directed them out of the sunny glare of the Avenida Atlantica and into the shade of the backstreets behind the hotel, ordering Luiz to stop near a service entrance. After a quick scan to check that the street was deserted, the boys in the back seat got out. Joker and Livio unloaded the suitcases from the boot, while Stripe stood guard, his AK-47 at his side. Angel got out of the car, his 12-gauge shotgun hidden within the folds of a long black trench coat, and walked around to Luiz's window.

'If the Doctor's given this the OK, the deal should be sweet, but I don't know this guy we're selling to and I certainly don't trust him. Wait here and keep your eyes open for any police. We're in Room 1412, which is at the back of the hotel. If you start hitting the horn, we'll hear it. Understand?'

Luiz nodded.

'Good.'

The *dono* of the Comando Negro swept towards the service entrance, his trench coat flapping in the breeze. The rest of his gang trailed after him, looking right and left along the street for any sign of trouble. They slipped through the service entrance and into the hotel, Stripe bringing up the rear.

Luiz stared out at the street, absent-mindedly toying with the GPS cross that Madison had given him. Now that he was outside the *favela*, he wondered whether Trojan Industries were following him – whether Madison or Jordan, or even Valerie, was watching him now. As ever, Luiz's thoughts turned to Ana. Jordan had promised he would try to arrange a meeting. Maybe once this deal was done, Luiz would phone Madison and push for a date.

A large black van pulled up by the hotel's service entrance, blocking his line of sight. Slinking down low in his seat, Luiz watched as the young driver got out. He was wearing blue workmen's overalls and had a bright green bandanna wrapped around his head. Walking to the back of the van, he opened the doors and a large group of boys began jumping down to the pavement. Although they were also dressed in overalls, they didn't look like any workmen Luiz had seen before and they were all sporting green accessories – bandannas, wristbands and baseball caps.

Green. The colour of the Quarto Comando – a violent *favela* gang, sworn enemies of the Comando Negro.

As each of the boys took a bulky Adidas holdall from the van and slung it over his shoulder, Luiz's heart was in his mouth. It was a classic gang tactic: there would be guns inside the sports bags, hidden from view but with their triggers in easy reach. Angel had walked straight into a trap.

Luiz jammed his finger down on the car horn.

Nothing happened.

He pressed it again, harder this time, but still to no avail. The car was so beat-up the horn didn't even work.

Swearing loudly, Luiz started the car and manoeuvred it away from the side of the road. With the Quarto Comando assembled at the rear of the building, he headed back on to Avenida Atlantica, coming to a screeching halt outside the main entrance of the Hotel Real. He left the car parked at an awkward angle, half on and half off the pavement, and sprinted past a line of ornamental trees into the lobby.

It was dark and cool inside, and it took a couple of seconds for Luiz's eyes to adjust to the light. He found himself in an open area tastefully decorated with plants in earthenware pots. Well-dressed businessmen lounged in plush armchairs, drinking cocktails with glamorous women in flowing dresses and large sunglasses. The hall was filled with the low buzz of polite conversation.

Luiz raced through the foyer, his flip-flops clattering across the marble floor, making for the main staircase beyond the reception desk. At the sight of the scruffily dressed boy, a porter in a brocaded uniform dropped the suitcase he was carrying and reached out to stop him. Pushing him away with the flat of his hand, Luiz hared up the staircase, ignoring the shouts that followed behind him.

As he ran through the carpeted hallways in search of Room 1412, Luiz quickly realized that the Hotel Real was a warren of identical corridors and rooms that appeared to have been numbered completely at random. He rounded a corner and nearly crashed into a maid, who screamed with surprise. Luiz shouted an apology over his shoulder, praying that the Quarto Comando were as lost as he was.

Sprinting up another flight of stairs, Luiz almost cried out in relief when he saw that Room 1412 was at the end of the corridor. He leaned against the door, panting, and hammered against it.

'It's me, Luiz!' he shouted. 'Open up!'

There was the sound of swearing inside and then the door opened, revealing MC Livio, a semi-automatic pistol in his hand. He carefully checked the corridor before beckoning Luiz inside.

Tucked away at the back of the hotel, Room 1412 clearly wasn't one of the plusher suites on offer. The blinds had been drawn and there was a thick smell of body odour in the air. Angel was sat at a low table with a fat man in a white linen suit, the *dono*'s shotgun resting near his left hand. There were three open suitcases on the table – two displaying bulky clear packets of cocaine, the other a vast wad of banknotes. Stripe was watching the window, while Joker stood in the doorway leading off to the bathroom.

There was a furious expression on Angel's face. 'What the hell are you doing here? I told you to wait in the car!'

'We've got to get out of here!' Luiz said breathlessly. 'It's a trap!'

'What are you talking about?'

'The Quarto Comando are on their way up here, maybe ten of them, and they're armed. We've got to go!'

Stripe trained his AK-47 on the fat businessman. 'You know anything about this?'

'Nothing!' the businessman shouted back, blanching. 'I never heard of the Quarto Comando!' He turned to Angel. 'What is this shit?'

Angel stood up grimly. 'It's nothing. We'll take care of it. We're done here anyway.'

The *dono* snapped shut the suitcase filled with money and passed it to MC Livio. With a final nod to the fat businessman, Angel picked up his shotgun and led his gang out of the hotel room.

As the Comando Negro filed into the corridor, tense fingers on triggers, there was a pinging sound behind them. Luiz turned to see the elevator doors at the end of the corridor opening and a flash of bright green . . .

14. Unwanted Guests

Angel didn't blink. Levelling his shotgun, he fired twice, punching two booming craters into the wall either side of the elevator. Surprised by the sudden ferocity of the attack, the Quarto Comando threw themselves against the sides of the lift. Stripe dropped to one knee and sprayed a round from his AK-47 at them, smashing the mirror on the back wall of the elevator to smithereens and keeping the gang members penned in until the doors trundled closed again.

'Let's get out of here!' Joker shouted, racing away down the hallway. As the Comando Negro followed after him, Luiz was suddenly painfully aware that he was the only gang member who wasn't carrying a weapon. If they got caught up in a firefight, how was he supposed to defend himself?

Joker skidded to a halt at the end of the corridor and peered round the corner. He pulled back sharply as bullets bit into the brickwork by his head.

'Shit!' he cried out, poking his gun around the corner and blindly firing off rounds. 'There's more here!'

'We're trapped!' Livio said despairingly.

'Good!' spat Stripe. 'I'm not running from these bastards anyway.'

Angel shook his head. 'They've got the jump on us and this place is going to be swarming with cops any minute. We gotta get out of here.'

Looking for an escape route, Luiz's eyes fell upon a pair of oak-panelled double doors on the other side of the hallway.

'Follow me!' he cried.

As he ran towards the doors, the elevator doors pinged open again, this time revealing the yawning barrel of a Heckler & Koch G3 assault rifle. Without breaking stride, Luiz threw himself against the double doors and raced down the long, straight corridor beyond, the footsteps of the Comando Negro following hot on his heels. Coming to a second set of double doors, he crashed through them – and into another world.

He was standing in a brightly lit dining room filled with hotel guests sitting down to lunch. The clink of crystal wine glasses and fine china could be heard above the soft jazz drifting out from the speakers. For a split second Luiz stood and stared at the diners, who stared back at him in astonishment, forks and spoons hovering by their mouths. Then came the sound of the G3 erupting in the corridor outside and the Comando Negro dived into the room.

That was when the screaming started.

Pandemonium broke out as the guests scattered – some diving under the tables, dragging their loved ones with them, while others stampeded for the exit. Some stayed in their chairs, rigid with shock. They watched as the Comando Negro battled through the crowds, leaving an obstacle course of tipped-over tables and chairs in their wake.

Someone shouted a warning – maybe Livio – and then the dining room exploded into gunfire as the Quarto Comando entered. They fired indiscriminately into the throng. Beside Luiz, a man fell to the floor, clutching his side and screaming in agony as blood welled from a gunshot wound. Luiz stopped, wanting to help, but Angel appeared out of the crowd and grabbed him by the arm, pushing him towards the flight of steps at the end of the dining room.

Glancing back over his shoulder, Luiz saw that Stripe was holding up the rear, reluctant to take a single backward step. Laughing maniacally as he unloaded his magazine at the rival gang, the *soldado*'s relentless stream of bullets scattered the Quarto Comando, forcing them to dive behind tables for cover.

'Stripe!' Angel bellowed above the uproar. 'Leave it!'

The guests had drained out of the dining room and were now flooding down the steps towards the lobby on a swell of screams and sobs. Angel followed them to the first floor, then gestured at the rest of his gang to come with him down a corridor.

'Where are you going?' Joker panted.

'There could be anyone waiting for us in the lobby,' Angel snarled. 'We'll go this way.'

Sprinting along the corridor, the *dono* came to a glass side door leading on to a terrace. He kicked it open and ran outside. The Comando Negro found themselves standing by a large swimming pool, its crystal blue waters lapping gently in the sunlight. The broad sweep of the Avenida Atlantica was just visible over a wall beyond the pool. There wasn't a soul in sight. The white sunloungers had been abandoned, leaving scattered towels as the only clue that anyone had been here. The sound of screaming still carried from inside the hotel to Luiz's ears, but it barely registered any more.

There was a flash of green from the side door of the hotel and then a blast of gunfire. Stripe spun round and shot back. There was a cry of pain and Luiz saw a smear of blood on the frame.

Angel pointed in the direction of the Avenida Atlantica. 'This way!'

Racing around the poolside, Luiz realized that the tiles were slick with water. He turned to warn Livio, but it was too late. The MC slipped over, sending the suitcase filled with money spiralling from his grasp. The Comando Negro watched as, in slow motion, the suitcase skidded towards the pool's edge. For a teasing second it teetered on the brink, before falling into the water with a splash.

'No!' cried Livio, scrambling on his hands and knees towards the pool.

Luiz dived behind a sunlounger as another round of bullets flew through the air. The Quarto Comando had hunkered down by the terrace door and were taking pot-shots at their exposed rivals. Luiz waited for a pause in the barrage, then darted out from the lounger and grabbed the MC.

'The money . . .!' Livio moaned.

'Screw the money!' Luiz screamed. 'Come on!'

He dragged Livio away from the poolside, trying to stay as low as possible. The rest of the Comando Negro were sheltering by the wall overlooking the Avenida Atlantica, from where they gave covering fire. As Luiz and Livio scurried towards them, Joker and Angel flipped themselves over the wall, negotiating the much steeper drop to the road on the other side. With one final blast of his AK-47, Stripe followed suit. The Quarto Comando opened fire again as Livio and Luiz reached the wall, diving headlong to safety as a hail of bullets flew above their heads.

Luiz hit the pavement hard, the air whooshing from his lungs on impact. Gingerly picking himself up, he saw a couple of tourists staring at him, fingers frozen on the buttons of their cameras. They watched dumbfounded as Luiz broke into a staggering run after the Comando Negro, who had spotted the battered Chevrolet mounted on the pavement outside the Hotel Real, and were racing back towards it.

Although there were no signs of any police on the Avenida Atlantica, the air was alive with the sound of sirens. As the gang piled into the car, Luiz started the engine. To his relief, it caught first time. Stamping down on the accelerator, he reversed straight into the traffic lane, amid clouds of smoke rising up from the tyres and the blaring horns of other motorists.

As Luiz urged the car off the main road and into the

backstreets that led to Santa Marta, Stripe punched the window. 'You fat IDIOT!' he screamed at Livio, who turned pale. 'You lost all the money!'

'Not now,' Angel rapped from the front seat, a deathly threat in his voice.

'Why not now, *dono*?' Stripe spat back. 'All he had to do was hold on to one lousy suitcase! We went through all that for *nothing*!'

'I said leave it.'

'You know who's got our money now? The Quarto Comando. Those bastards'll be pissing themselves laughing –'

Distracted, Luiz didn't see the black van come veering out from an alleyway until the last second. As the van headed straight for the side of their car, Luiz yanked on the steering wheel. The car mounted the pavement, clattering through a couple of empty tables outside a restaurant and missing the van's bumper by a matter of inches.

'What the hell was that?' someone shouted, as Luiz jammed down on the accelerator.

'It's the Quarto Comando!' Luiz shouted back.

'Keep going for the *boca*,' urged Angel. 'They won't dare take us on there.'

'The car won't make it that far,' Luiz said, through gritted teeth. The ominous silhouette of the black van was blocking out the sun in his rear-view mirror and he wasn't sure how much more speed he could squeeze out of the engine.

'Shut up and drive!' Stripe snarled. 'I'll take care of the van.'

The blond-haired boy leaned out of the back passenger window and aimed his AK-47 at the van, peppering the grille with bullets.

As they raced through the Zona Sul back towards Santa Marta, Luiz had to channel every ounce of concentration into keeping the Chevrolet on the road, the fragile suspension shuddering as they bounced over bumps and potholes. He swerved in and out of traffic, forcing other drivers to jam on their brakes to avoid a collision, all the while the van looming on their tail like a nightmare. Hunched low in their seats, the rest of the gang continued to fire off shots at their pursuers, the reports so loud and continuous that Luiz could barely hear himself think. But even though the front of the Quarto Comando's van was now riddled with bullet holes, the driver never let up for a second.

The Chevrolet's engine growled in protest as the road began to climb and Luiz realized that they were on the familiar approach back to Santa Marta.

'We're going to make it!' Livio cried out.

At the sight of the car careering up the hill, the lookouts near the *boca* began shouting into their radio phones. All around them kites were dropping from the sky like stones. As the *boca* loomed into view, Luiz offered up a silent prayer that the lookouts had recognized the car and he wasn't driving them straight into another hail of bullets. He could see the guards scrambling into firing positions. As the car drew into range, Luiz hardly dared breathe.

The guards held their fire, waiting until the black van

was in sight before unleashing a storm of bullets over the top of Luiz's car at their pursuers. There was a loud squeal of brakes.

'They're backing off!' Stripe called out jubilantly.

Before Luiz could celebrate, there was a loud pop and one of the front tyres blew out. Struggling to control the Chevrolet as it careered into a spin up the narrowing road, the last thing he saw was the guards scattering out of the way like ninepins and then the car ploughed straight into the *boca*.

15. Inquests

Luiz groggily raised his head. The impact of the crash had sent him flying forward into the steering wheel and he could feel a trickle of blood running down the side of his face. Through the shattered windscreen, Luiz could see the wall of the *boca*, dominated by a giant Comando Negro tag. As a cloud of dust and smoke enveloped him, he coughed. The smell of oil and burnt rubber was everywhere.

For a while nobody in the car spoke and then, from the back seat, came the sound of chuckling laughter.

'No way, man!' whooped Joker. 'That was *insane!*'

He clapped his hands together with glee and clambered monkey-like out of the car. The *boca* guards had formed a cautious semicircle around the vehicle, peering into the wreckage. When Angel appeared unharmed, there was an audible murmur of relief.

Luiz was the last to get out. His head pounding, he found Livio mournfully inspecting the damage. The front of the car had buckled on impact, the bonnet flying upwards to expose the mangled innards of engine parts. The MC looked inconsolable.

'What's up? You don't really care about this shitheap, do you?'

'I don't,' Livio lamented, 'but my cousin will. It's his car.'

Luiz burst out laughing and hugged the MC.

'Tell him we'll buy him a new one,' Joker shouted, pretending to count out the loose change in his pocket. 'I got more than enough here.'

As the crowd around them laughed and began patting him on the back, Luiz couldn't deny the thrill of the adrenalin surging through his veins. They had come very close to dying, but everyone had made it back alive – and it had been almost entirely down to him.

'Quarto Comando can kiss my ass!'

Joker bent over and dropped his shorts, exposing his backside down the hill, towards where the black van had long since retreated. 'You see that, you pussies?'

The gang members around him burst out laughing, adding their taunts and catcalls to the chorus. Someone up on the roof fired a couple of shots into the air, while the boys began bouncing up and down on their toes, chanting and throwing their arms around one another's shoulders. Even Stripe struggled to hold back a grin.

One person wasn't laughing.

'Pull up your shorts and let's go. We've got things to discuss.'

Angel said it quietly, but his words carried over the *boca*. Immediately the chanting petered out. Joker hastily hitched up his shorts and followed his brother as he strode away into Santa Marta.

'So . . . what the hell happened back there?'

The five of them had congregated in Angel's front room: Luiz, Livio, Stripe, Joker and the *dono* himself. Having never been inside the *dono*'s house before, Luiz was surprised to find that it wasn't much bigger than the place Livio was letting him sleep in. Noticing his appraisal of the surroundings, the MC nudged Luiz in the ribs.

'Ain't no fancy hotels in this *favela*, my friend,' he whispered. 'And with the amount of girlfriends Angel's got, he needs to earn every cent.'

As Joker fetched beers from the fridge, Livio immediately sat down to roll a joint. Stripe produced a large packet of cocaine from one of his pockets and began chopping up lines on a tray on his knees, while Angel disappeared into the bedroom. It wasn't long before Luiz heard raised voices, then a statuesque black woman in a tiny white skirt and bra top stalked past them and out of the house without a word. The flimsy bedroom wall shook as something was hurled against it, the sound of breaking glass carrying through to the front room, and then Angel reappeared, muttering under his breath and demanding a joint from Livio.

Now the air was thick with the smell of marijuana – and Angel's pregnant question.

'Some bastard set us up,' Livio said finally, exhaling a

cloud of smoke into the air. 'Those guys were waiting for us. They had come prepared, man.'

'What about the guy who was buying the blow from us?' asked Joker. 'You think he had anything to do with it?'

Angel shook his head and took a sip from his beer. 'That guy didn't have the balls for anything like that. Anyway, he came with a reference from the Doctor. You think *he* set us up?'

'I don't know, Angel. You're the only guy who's met him,' said Livio.

The *dono* gave him a hard stare. 'The only thing you need to know is that the Doctor is the only reason the Comando Negro exists. You're more likely to sell us out than he is.'

'Hey – I'm no rat!' the MC protested.

Stripe loudly snorted a line of cocaine, throwing his head back as the drug coursed through his system.

'I don't know why you're wasting all this time bitching,' he said matter-of-factly, pinching his nostrils with his fingers. 'It's obvious there's a rat and it's obvious who he is.'

'Really?' said Angel. 'Who?'

'It's Luiz.'

Luiz had been expecting this from the start. Of course Stripe was going to blame him. He schooled his expression to one of amused bafflement.

'Are you crazy, Stripe?' Joker asked, tapping the side of his head with a finger. 'Didn't you see Luiz driving the car?'

'Look, it's simple,' Stripe maintained. 'This has never happened to us before. There's only one guy we don't know. It has to be Luiz.'

'Hey!' Livio cut in. 'Luiz is Comando Negro! We know him!'

'We don't know *shit* about him,' Stripe retorted, pointing a finger at Luiz. 'I don't know where he's from or who his family is. The only thing I know is that he can drive and Livio thinks the sun shines out of his ass.'

Stripe was getting dangerously close to the truth here. Luiz kept his mouth shut, his attention fixed on the one man who hadn't said anything. Angel took a thoughtful swig from his beer bottle, wiping his mouth with the back of his hand.

'If Luiz hadn't warned us in the hotel, we'd have walked out of that room into a firing squad. And then he managed to drive that shitheap all the way back to Santa Marta. I know what I need to know about him. He isn't a rat.'

It was a struggle for Luiz to keep the relief from flickering across his face. Stripe began to protest.

'OK, so he warned us in the hotel and he drove us home. But whenever there's shooting to be done, real *soldado* work, I don't see him picking up a gun.' His eyes narrowed. 'Are you scared to pull the trigger or afraid you'd hit one of your gang buddies?'

'Enough!' roared Angel.

His arm whipped out like a striking cobra, flipping Stripe's tray into his face. As a spray of cocaine went up in the air, Angel smashed his bottle over Stripe's blond head.

Stripe crumpled to the floor, with the *dono* on him in an instant. From nowhere a small gun had appeared in his left hand, which he jammed underneath Stripe's chin. With his right hand, Angel reached down and pulled out a handful of cocaine from the opened packet, rubbing the powder in the boy's face.

'I'm tired of your shit!' he bellowed. 'You hear me? You stick so much cocaine up your nose everyone's your enemy. Dog, Luiz . . . Who's next, tough guy? You going to come after me? Hey?'

Stripe thrashed and writhed on the floor, his face smeared with a mixture of blood and cocaine. The rest of the Comando Negro looked on in shocked silence.

'Would you shoot me, Angel?' Stripe said, his voice choked.

'In a heartbeat,' the *dono* replied softly.

For a few seconds the room held its breath. Then Angel slowly removed his gun from underneath Stripe's chin, standing up and moving back into his chair. Stripe staggered to his feet, tears in his eyes. He turned on Luiz.

'You don't fool me,' he said. 'You're a rat and I'm going to prove it.'

Clutching his bleeding head, Stripe stumbled out through the door and began running down the street. As the rest of the gang watched him go, Livio blew out his cheeks and clapped Luiz on the back.

'Don't take it personally, man. Stripe gets wired when he does too much cocaine. He'll calm down.'

'He'd better do,' Angel said in a deathly quiet voice, 'or I'm going to blow him away.'

It was two o'clock in the morning and Luiz was having trouble falling asleep. His mind was still racing from the events of the day and the muggy atmosphere wasn't helping him relax. A sour odour of urine hung in the air, and every now and again he heard the squeaking and scrabbling of a rat as it scampered across the floor. The couple in the shack next door were having a violent argument, their shouts echoing through the thin walls.

Already tense, Luiz jumped with surprise as his phone started to vibrate. It was Ricardo's Pizzeria. They were calling him. He pressed the 'Answer' button.

'Hello?'

'Luiz?' Richard Madison's voice was low and urgent. 'Is it safe to talk?'

'Yeah. I'm alone.'

'The gunfight at the hotel was all over the news. Are you all right? What the hell happened?'

'We got set up. The Doctor had organized a drug deal, but someone told the Quarto Comando. It was a miracle we made it back to Santa Marta.'

'Did you get hurt?'

'No – I'm OK. But I did see a guy get shot at the hotel,' Luiz said softly. 'Is he all right?'

'He's in hospital. He should pull through. Another old lady had a heart attack and she's in intensive care. It's amazing that there weren't more casualties. But one of the Quarto Comando was killed in the fighting.'

Luiz thought back to the hotel poolside, and the cry of pain and the smear of blood in the doorway. He had witnessed someone getting killed. The thought sent a chill down his spine.

'Councillor Jorge Cruz has been all over the media, calling on the police to launch a raid into Santa Marta. Given the amount of attention being paid to the Comando Negro, it's becoming difficult for us to stay invisible. Darius is talking about calling a halt to the operation.'

'What? He can't! Not after all this!'

'I know. Valerie and I are trying to talk him round. I'll let you know as soon as I know for definite. And one more thing.'

'What?'

There was a pause at the end of the line. 'You keep saying "we". "We" got set up. "We" made it back. I know you're trying to fit in, but remember who these guys are, Luiz. They're not your friends.'

'I know.'

But even as he paced around the threadbare room trying to reassure Madison, with rain beginning to fall on the dusty *favela* roads outside, it felt to Luiz like he was speaking to someone very far away, from another world.

16. Party Time

Early the next afternoon, Luiz made his way through Santa Marta, heading towards Livio's house. If he didn't yet feel entirely at ease within the *favela*, at least he had lost the dreadful fear of discovery that had haunted his every step during the first few days. Here and there he even recognized a familiar face – received a nod of recognition back from the Comando Negro members milling about on the *favela* street corners.

After the phone call from Madison, Luiz was more concerned about Trojan Industries. Perhaps he should have felt relieved at the thought that Jordan might call the whole thing off, but then there was no telling what would happen to Ana. Luiz didn't trust Trojan enough to think that they'd help free her out of the goodness of their hearts. Her best hope was that Luiz could somehow successfully complete his mission.

Wrapped up in his thoughts, Luiz didn't see the little boy shuffling along the shady part of the street until the last minute.

'Hey, Dog!' he called out. 'Wait up!'

The boy glanced up fearfully at the sound of his name.

Even though a few days had passed since the football match, Dog still bore the scars of Stripe's assault: his nose was bent out of shape and the flesh around his right eye had swollen and turned an ugly purple.

Having given him a friendly wave, Luiz was surprised to see Dog break into a scuttling run down the nearest side alley. Briefly he thought about going after him, then decided against it. All of the Comando Negro knew Santa Marta like the back of their hand and Luiz wasn't going to risk getting lost in the maze. Anyway, after what had happened to Dog, it was hard to blame the boy for wanting to avoid other gang members.

Arriving at the MC's shack, Luiz was surprised to find that he was interrupting a family meal. Livio was trying to coax a little girl into eating another spoonful of food, while his wife rocked a crying baby in her arms, whispering gentle hushes into its ears. The MC gestured for Luiz to come in, a smile wreathed across his face.

'Luiz! Come in, man. Meet my wife, Gabriela.'

Livio's wife was probably the same age as Luiz – a small, dark teenager with serious eyes. As Luiz greeted her, Gabriela smiled politely back, but there was no warmth in it. She warily ushered the little girl into the adjoining bedroom and carried the baby in with her, closing the door behind them.

Livio noticed Luiz's concerned expression. 'Don't worry about Gabriela. The stuff with the Quarto Comando's got her a bit jumpy, that's all.'

'Why's that?'

The MC shook his head. 'Don't you get it, man? They tried to kill Angel! He's not just going to sit there and take it! And we still got problems with the Compadres too. There's going to be some serious shit going down in the next few days, believe me.'

'You going to be involved?'

Livio shrugged. 'I'm Comando Negro, aren't I?'

'I'm guessing Gabriela wishes you weren't.'

'She's living in a dreamworld,' the MC shot back, getting up from the table. '*This* is real, all this right here.' Suddenly animated, Livio strode over to the wall of his shack and scratched a fingernail across it. A crumbly powder of brickwork broke off, which he rubbed between his fingers. 'The walls in this place are falling down, Luiz! All the houses in Santa Marta are like this: mine, Stripe's, Angel's ... It doesn't matter who you are in the *favela*, this is the best you get. You don't think I want better for my family?'

The MC collapsed into a chair and cracked open a bottle of Skol. He frowned.

'You ever see those houses on the other side of town? The big ones with all the gates and the guards?'

Luiz nodded. Rio's wealthy inhabitants tended to hide as far away from the *favelas* as possible, in gated compounds protected by round-the-clock security. Livio sighed.

'That's where I want to live, my friend. Kick back in a swimming pool all day, not having to worry about money or any of that shit. I barely got enough to keep my kids in clothes! You ever hear that Councillor Cruz on the TV calling us animals? You think his walls are falling down? A greedy politician like him, filling his pockets whenever he can? I grew up with nothing. I'm going to die with nothing. No one's going to help me. I've got to help myself. If that means I've got to pull the trigger, then so be it.'

Livio broke off to take a moody swig from his bottle. Surprised by the passion of his outburst, Luiz was unsure what to say. After a pregnant silence, the MC snorted to himself and waved a dismissive hand.

'Ignore me. I get carried away sometimes.' A grin stole over Livio's face. 'Enough speeches, man. Let's go have some *fun.*'

The pickup truck hurtled through the *favela*, homing in on the thundering bassline that was booming out over Santa Marta in a series of sonic explosions. Sitting in the back of the vehicle, Luiz laughed as the truck bounced wildly over a pothole, sending him tumbling to the floor. Beside him, Livio pointed and laughed.

'Bet you wish you were driving now, asshole!' he crowed.

Luiz's cheeks were flushed and his head was giddy from the beer he had drunk. Livio had made it clear that he expected Luiz to keep him company through the afternoon – refusing would only have made him stand out. As the hours had passed and the rest of the Comando Negro command had joined them, for the first time since returning to Santa Marta Luiz's mission had slipped from his mind. Now they were heading for a *baile-funk* party over on the far side of the *favela*, which Livio had promised would be filled with *popozudas* – pretty girls with curvy asses. It was Joker peering out into the darkness behind the wheel of the truck, while his elder brother sat alongside him.

As their destination came into view – a large shack to the east of Santa Marta – Livio whooped with delight. The corrugated-iron walls were shaking to the vibrations of the bass, as though at any moment the music might bring the roof crashing down around everyone's ears. It was immediately apparent that the Comando Negro had provided security for the party – two boys dressed in black were standing by the front door, assault rifles cradled in their arms. As Angel got out from the front passenger seat, he nodded at the guards, then marched briskly past them into the club.

Walking inside, Luiz was assailed by a maelstrom of noise. The room was pitch black, the darkness punctuated by a firestorm of red strobe lights that gave people's faces an eerie glow whenever it fell upon them. On the stage two DJs were hunched over banks of mixing desks, while an MC rapped over the harsh loops.

The reaction to the Comando Negro's entrance was immediate. A cheer went up from the crowd and the MC pointed to them, shouting out a greeting. Two younger boys bounced towards Luiz, making the shape of the letters 'C' and 'N' with their fingers in celebration of the gang. Someone thrust another beer bottle into his hand, patting him on the back. Although most people went out of their way to greet the Comando Negro and be friendly with them, Luiz couldn't help noticing the others – the young people who stepped out of their way, heads bowed, fearfully refusing to make eye contact. Although part of Luiz wanted to tell them that he was different, that he wasn't a violent killer, another part of him felt a guilty thrill of power. He thought of Dog – suddenly it seemed entirely understandable that the little boy wanted to be a part of this, no matter what it would end up costing him.

The dance floor was so jammed it looked as though the entire population of Santa Marta had tried to fit into the one room. Luiz couldn't help but notice the girls, who had apparently prepared for the cramped, steamy conditions by wearing as little as possible. They were grinding their bodies in time with the beat, their bare midriffs glistening with sweat.

A hand clamped down on Luiz's shoulder. Angel watched the girls dancing, taking long drags on a thick cigar.

'You'll have fun tonight, Luiz,' he said, grinning, his white teeth gleaming in the darkness. 'Make sure you find yourself a good woman. You're Comando Negro, remember? We got a reputation to uphold.'

With that, the *dono* patted his cheek and walked off. Luiz was suddenly aware that he was on his own. Livio had vanished, while Joker was happily surrounded by a ring of admiring girls, who listened spellbound as he retold the story of the showdown at the Hotel Real.

'So there's bullets flying everywhere and my man Luiz is driving like Felipe Massa ...' Here Joker slipped in an impersonation of the Formula One driver steering round a hairpin. 'It was a miracle we got out, I'm telling you.'

His story was interrupted by a massive roar of approval from the crowd. Luiz turned round to see Livio taking the stage. The MC was dressed in baggy desert-camouflage shorts and a Portuguese football shirt with 'Ronaldo' written on the back. Microphone in hand, he prowled across the stage, like a big cat marking out its territory. Then, as the beats behind him began to intensify, he broke into a low growling rap that got the crowd yelling and screaming in appreciation. The laid-back family man from earlier in the day had completely vanished. Luiz could only marvel at his friend's transformation.

As he stood at the side of the dance floor watching the MC, Luiz noticed a girl smiling at him. He recognized her instantly. It was Marie – the girl who had been at the five-a-side game. Dressed only in a red bikini top and a pair of tiny cut-off denim shorts, she looked a different girl from the one who had watched him so shyly from the side-lines.

Marie broke away from her friends and glided towards him, her thumbs resting in the belt loops of her shorts. She gave Luiz a cat-like grin and wrapped her slender arms around his neck, enveloping him in a subtle wisp of perfume.

'I was hoping you were going to come,' she said.

'Yeah?' replied Luiz. 'Why's that?'

'I wanted to talk to Santa Marta's new hero. First you saved Dog's life and now Angel himself. You're the talk of the *favela*.'

Luiz shrugged. 'I think Angel can take care of himself. I was just driving the car.'

'Modest too.' Marie smiled. She kissed him softly on the cheek and whispered in his ear, 'Let's get out of here.'

A voice at the back of Luiz's mind was telling him that this wasn't a good idea, but at that moment – with the music overwhelming him, the alcohol racing through his system and the beautiful girl smiling at him – it seemed impossible to say no. As he and Marie walked hand in hand out of the club, Livio was barking like a dog into the microphone. He had been joined on stage by a woman in a flimsy dress who was shaking her ass in time to the beat, each grinding movement sending the bottom of her dress flicking up to reveal a flash of white thong. The boys in the crowd were cheering and holding up their camera phones, squabbling among one another as they tried to take the best picture of her.

After the mayhem of the club, the night felt very still and quiet outside. Wordlessly moving past the guards and into the shadows of a deserted alleyway, Luiz and Marie drew closer together and began to kiss. As he felt the soft touch of the girl's lips upon his, Luiz was dimly aware of the club door crashing open and footsteps making unsteady progress towards them. They came to a halt near the end of the alleyway and then a voice spoke into a phone.

'I can talk now,' said Angel. 'There's no one around.'

Even though the *dono*'s voice was slightly slurred, there was a deferential tone that Luiz hadn't heard before. Marie didn't seem to have registered Angel's proximity – smoothly, Luiz pressed her closer against the wall and further into the shadows.

'I don't know what happened,' Angel continued. 'Somebody squealed to the Quarto Comando about the deal. I don't know who yet, but I'll find out. I guarantee you that, Doctor.'

The hairs on the back of Luiz's neck stood up at the word 'Doctor'. Still kissing Marie, he strained to catch the rest of the conversation.

'Yeah – I'll meet you tomorrow. Where? The Casa Bahia? OK, I'll see you at four.'

With that, Angel turned off his phone and lurched back towards the club. Luiz couldn't believe it. The Doctor was going to be at a meeting tomorrow, and Luiz knew when and where.

'What's wrong?'

Finally noticing his distraction, Marie had stopped kissing him and was now looking at him curiously. Luiz smiled, brushing a strand of hair away from her face.

'Nothing,' he replied, drawing her close to him again. 'Nothing at all.'

17. Casa Bahia

The sunshine beamed down on the glamorous district of Ipanema, dappling the leaves of the trees that lined its broad thoroughfares. Here in the heart of the Zona Sul, there were juice bars and cafes on every corner, providing rest and refreshment for the tourists and rich *cariocas* who browsed through the local boutiques, their arms laden with shopping bags.

Walking through the well-dressed crowds in his gang clothes – shorts and sandals, long basketball shirt and a cap – Luiz stuck out like a sore thumb. At that moment, he couldn't care less. The bright sunshine was hurting his eyes and he was suffering from a throbbing headache and parched mouth. That was the last time he was going to drink so much beer, he decided.

To try and avoid suspicion, Luiz had stayed with Marie for a while in the alleyway, before making his excuses and walking her home. She had seemed disappointed that the night had ended so early, but the *dono*'s conversation had provided Luiz with a sharp reminder of his mission priorities. Now was not the time to be getting involved with a girl, no matter how pretty she was. Luiz found himself wondering what Marie would have done if she had known the truth about him – would she still have kissed him, or spat in his face and told the Comando Negro?

Luiz's feelings about his deception were becoming more complex by the day. At first he had just been terrified of the gang finding out and killing him, putting him in the microwave, but now there were other, more complicated problems. What would Livio do if he found out? What would the rest of the gang do to Livio? After all, it was the MC who had introduced Luiz to Santa Marta, taken care of him, vouched for him in front of the Comando Negro. If Luiz was unmasked as a spy, would Livio also end up paying the ultimate price?

Shaking his head to clear away the dark thoughts, Luiz turned the corner and found himself on Rua Redentor, an upmarket road several streets back from Ipanema Beach. Up ahead, the bright blue awning of the Casa Bahia was rippling in the breeze. Boasting a reputation as one of the best restaurants in Rio, the Casa Bahia was not the kind of place you expected a member of the Comando Negro to visit. Luiz and Ana had been taken there once by their foster parents, to celebrate the first anniversary of their adoption. Luiz could still remember the rich smell of pork sizzling up from the kitchens and the sound of the samba band playing in the background.

Crossing the road, he ordered a drink at the juice bar opposite the restaurant and sat down at a table partly obscured by a large fern. He checked his watch – it was quarter to four. Having called Ricardo's Pizzeria earlier in the day and ordered another large pizza with black olives, Luiz had been able to arrange a meeting with someone from Trojan now. When Luiz first caught sight of Juan Oliveira's leather jacket, he was simply relieved that he wasn't Valerie Singer. But as the large policeman neared, Luiz realized how dangerous this meeting could be. He slunk down low in his chair and pulled his baseball cap over his face.

Oliveira took a seat across the table from Luiz and made himself comfortable.

'You look like shit,' he said, a flicker of amusement on his face. 'Rough night?'

Luiz pulled a face, but didn't reply. The policeman looked up and down the street, nodding approvingly.

'You've chosen a good spot here. We've got a great view of the restaurant entrance, but that fern should give us cover if anyone is looking out for us.'

'It better had do,' Luiz replied. 'If they see me sitting out here with a policeman, I'm dead. Couldn't you have just bugged the restaurant or something?'

Oliveira laughed. 'It's not quite that simple, Luiz. I've had enough trouble trying to explain how a police station door got shot through during your little breakout. I start requesting bugs on top of that and people are going to be asking questions. Especially since your little firework display down at the hotel. You don't make life easy for yourself, do you?'

'It wasn't like I was the one who opened fire!' Luiz protested. 'It was a trap!'

'Well, anyway, low-key is better. If I know our man Angel, he's going to have his eyes peeled for anything suspicious and this could be our only chance to get a lead on the Doctor. I don't want anything messing it up.'

The policeman got up to order a starfruit *carimbola* drink, while Luiz slowly sipped his orange juice, the cool liquid soothing his dry mouth.

Suddenly he shrank back behind the fern.

'What is it?' Oliveira asked crisply, as he returned to the table.

'Angel!' hissed Luiz.

Although the *dono* of the Comando Negro had changed out of his usual clothes into a smart black shirt and chinos, there was no mistaking his giant, dreadlocked frame as he strode down Rua Redentor. Angel moved with a powerful grace, his eyes glancing warily around him.

As the *dono* approached the restaurant, Juan Oliveira pulled out a camera and began snapping calmly over Luiz's shoulder at the front of the Casa Bahia.

'Look like you're enjoying yourself, son,' he murmured. 'I'm going to be taking a lot of photos of you this afternoon.'

Luiz adopted a frozen smile, all the while fighting the urge to duck under the table.

'I'm not sure how much Angel trusts the good Doctor,' Oliveira said thoughtfully. 'He's strapped.'

'He's carrying a gun? How can you tell?'

'After twenty years, you just can.'

Risking a peek over his shoulder, Luiz saw that a man

was standing in the doorway of the restaurant, blocking Angel's path.

'Who's that?' Luiz said excitedly. 'Is it . . .?'

Oliveira shook his head.

'I'm afraid not. That's Ivan Fernandes. He owns the Casa Bahia.'

Ivan Fernandes was a small, blond-haired man with a close-cropped beard. Dressed in a flamboyant pink shirt, he flicked off a fleck of dirt from his cuffs as Angel approached. Even though the *dono* towered over him, Fernandes didn't seem intimidated. For a minute, Luiz thought that the restaurant owner was going to stop Angel from entering, but at the last second he stepped aside and gestured for the gang member to enter.

It was five to four. Luiz could feel his excitement growing. If he was right, then any moment now the Doctor was going to walk past them. If they could identify him, then Luiz's mission would be over. Ana could be free before night fell.

'Another one coming,' Oliveira reported.

Luiz clutched the policeman's arm in shock.

'Hang on a second,' he gasped. 'That's Fabio!'

One of the most famous actors in Brazil, Fabio was the star of a new *novela* – a soap opera – which had millions of people tuning in their televisions six nights a week. Luiz hated the *novelas* himself and was always teasing Ana for watching them. Even so, it was a surprise to see such a famous man in the flesh.

His face partially obscured by a large pair of aviator

sunglasses, Fabio glanced up and down the street before hurrying inside the Casa Bahia.

'Idiot,' scoffed Oliveira.

'What is it?'

'He's trying to look unremarkable, but everything he's doing says "look at me". If you want people to ignore you, Luiz, you gotta be Mr Grey, Mr Average. Our friend Fabio is about as inconspicuous as an elephant in a tutu.'

'There's no way he could be involved, is there?'

Oliveira snorted dismissively. 'That clothes-horse? Not a chance. My guess is he's cheating on his girlfriend. Or his boyfriend.'

They waited for more people to arrive at the restaurant, but the entrance remained quiet. Luiz glanced down at his watch. It was nearly quarter past four – and no one had come in or out of the restaurant since Fabio.

'Maybe the Doctor's not coming,' he said. 'Maybe –'

'Ssh – look.'

A silver BMW with tinted windows had pulled up outside the Casa Bahia. Two bodyguards sprang out from the side of the car and opened the rear passenger door. A round, bald figure got out from the BMW, dabbing at his forehead with a white handkerchief.

Oliveira let out a low whistle.

'Seems like it's our day to spot celebrities.'

As the bald man spun round to bark orders at a subordinate, Luiz recognized him instantly.

It was Councillor Jorge Cruz.

*

Luiz gaped at the councillor as he brushed down the front of his suit and stomped inside the restaurant. His body-guards checked the street behind him, their hands hovering by the insides of their jackets, where their gun holsters would be. Undeterred, Oliveira casually fired off a couple of photographs with Luiz in the foreground, before returning to his *carimbola*.

'It doesn't make any sense!' Luiz hissed, leaning forward over the table. 'Cruz *can't* be the Doctor! He spends all his time going on about how evil the Comando Negro are – if he's involved, wouldn't he keep his mouth shut?'

'Perhaps.' Oliveira shrugged. 'His reputation does give him cover, though.'

'You really think it could be him?'

'I'm not sure. But let's just say it wouldn't be the first corrupt politician in Rio's history,' Oliveira said grimly.

After Cruz had disappeared inside the restaurant, Luiz and Oliveira remained at the juice bar. For the first time, Luiz had a sense of what stake-outs must be like outside of the movies. He sat there with the policeman, staring at the same patch of pavement, unable even to see through the windows of the restaurant into the shady interior.

Luiz was almost falling asleep when Oliveira suddenly stiffened, and he saw that Angel had come striding back out of the Casa Bahia. The *dono* lit up a cigarette, tossing his match to the ground near the entrance. There was a movement in the restaurant doorway and Ivan Fernandes appeared. The little restaurant owner pointedly picked up the match, exchanging an unfriendly glance with Angel.

Luiz was worried that the *dono* was going to pull out his gun, but then Angel snorted with laughter and turned on his heel. Fernandes watched him walk away, the gang leader a head taller than nearly everyone else in the crowd.

'That guy's got some balls,' Luiz muttered. 'Not many people stare down Angel like that.'

'Fernandes is legendarily proud of his restaurant,' Oliveira said, chuckling. 'It doesn't look like he's going to be welcoming Angel back any time soon.'

It was another half an hour before Councillor Cruz followed the Comando Negro *dono* out of the door, surrounded by his coterie of bodyguards. He was escorted into the back of the silver BMW, which then flew away from the kerb in a squeal of tyres.

As the car disappeared down Rua Redentor, Luiz, sore from hours sitting in the same seat, stood up and stretched languidly.

'So they've gone. What now?'

'I'm going back to the station,' the policeman replied. 'I'll see what I can dig up on Cruz – if there are any links to the Comando Negro. Maybe I'll strike lucky. I'm guessing you're going back to Santa Marta. Hold on a moment.'

Oliveira reached inside the pocket of his leather jacket and pulled out a vibrating mobile phone. He listened carefully as someone spoke to him at length.

'OK,' he said finally. 'I'll take care of it. Thanks for the heads-up.'

The policeman snapped his mobile phone shut, a thoughtful expression on his face.

'Change of plan?' asked Luiz.

Oliveira nodded. 'Looks like you may not need to go back to Santa Marta after all,' he said. 'That was one of my colleagues. We've got a guy from the Comando Negro who claims he can identify the Doctor. I'm going to speak to him now – see if he's for real.'

'Really? Where?'

'Polinter prison,' replied Oliveira, a shadow crossing his face as he spoke.

18. Prison Break

Oliveira drove through Rio's downtown traffic in an unmarked red car, visibly unhappy at the presence of Luiz alongside him. When the boy had first suggested accompanying him to the prison, the policeman had flatly refused.

'No way,' he said. 'You have no idea what it's like in there. And, believe me, you don't want to.'

'I don't care!' Luiz shot back. 'Let me come with you. Then I can check this guy out and see if he's on the level.'

Oliveira raised an eyebrow. 'You worried I might get hoodwinked by one of these geniuses?'

'I'm the one who's been hanging out with the Comando Negro, not you. I'll be able to tell you in a second if he's bullshitting. You need me there!'

'It's not safe. Jesus, Luiz, I can't take a kid with me into Polinter!'

'The prisoners are behind bars, aren't they? Anyway, you'll be with me.' Luiz paused before continuing quietly, 'Look, the sooner we find out who the Doctor is, the sooner I can get Ana out of the police station. She's not going to spend one more second in there than she has to.'

Oliveira muttered something under his breath.

'You're as bad as Jordan, you know that?' he said finally.

'It's my sister, Juan,' Luiz replied simply. 'Would you sit around and wait?'

The policeman blew out his cheeks and reluctantly gestured towards his car. Now they drove in a tense silence, neither of them sure what to say to the other.

'So why's this guy talking, anyway?' Luiz asked eventually, as the car came to a stop at traffic lights. 'If word gets out that he's informing on the Comando Negro, they'll kill him in a heartbeat.'

'Well, he's not doing it out of the goodness of his heart. In exchange for the information, he wants us to get him out of Polinter.'

'And will you?'

'If he leads us to the Doctor, I'll unlock the cell door myself. But I'll believe it when I see it. These guys are full of bullshit – they'll do anything to get out. You're right about one thing, though: the informer's not safe. There's almost as many gang members in Rio's prisons as there are in the *favelas*.' Oliveira turned in his seat to look at Luiz. 'You want to understand the gangs in Rio, you gotta understand the prisons, son. If you're not a gang member when you go inside, chances are you will be by the time you come out. You don't survive these sorts of places on your own. The Compadres actually began in prison. So did the Quarto Comando. Being a new gang, the Comando Negro are badly outnumbered in Polinter, and that's not a good situation to be in.'

'They'd better stay out of prison, then.'

'Believe me when I say that your pals in the Comando Negro will end up one of two ways: lying face down in the dirt with a bullet in their head or here. Either way, they're screwed. In prison, quite literally.'

'There's no hope for them?'

'Put it this way: you seen any old gangsters walking around Santa Marta, holding up people with their canes?'

Luiz fell silent. The policeman had a point.

'Look,' Oliveira continued. 'I'm not saying that I don't understand their position. These kids have got no money, no education, no prospects. If you're rich and live in Rio, you live like a king. If you're poor, you live like shit. But that doesn't give you the right to go around robbing and shooting people.'

'Not everyone in the Comando Negro is a bad guy,' Luiz protested. 'Guys like Livio are OK – they just don't think they've got any choice. It's not like anyone outside of the *favela* is going to give them a job.'

Oliveira raised an eyebrow. 'Well, I live in Borel *favela* and I don't deal drugs.'

'*You* live in a *favela*? But you're a cop!'

'You noticed?' Oliveira replied, laughing.

'I mean – how come no one's tried to kill you?'

'Because no one knows what I do. I keep the badge hidden until I get outside of Borel. Like I say, Luiz, there's always a choice.'

Casting his mind back, Luiz remembered Jordan saying something similar when they met. Not for the first time, he was struck by the fluid lines between right and wrong in Rio – the corrupt politicians, the friendly gang members, the 'black ops' organization that had forced him to go back to Santa Marta. He had a sneaking suspicion that the gruff policeman was in fact the best of them all.

Oliveira indicated left and drove into Polinter's car park. From the outside, the prison – a small, nondescript white building in the centre of Rio – looked like nothing more than an office block. A queue of people had formed outside for visiting hours, their arms folded and their faces subdued.

Oliveira parked the car, then reached into his glove compartment and handed Luiz a black balaclava. 'Put this on.'

'Why?'

'Polinter's filled with gang members, remember? Do you really want word getting back to the Comando Negro that you're walking round with a cop?'

'Oh, right.'

Luiz put on the balaclava, suddenly feeling very self-conscious. He scurried after Oliveira as the policeman marched past the waiting queue and through the main entrance, flashing his badge at the guards at the security check. A couple of the guards nodded at him in recognition.

They made their way deep into the bowels of the building, until the sunlight was replaced by a fetid gloom. The final checkpoint was at the end of a long corridor, where two men were standing guard at a door, pump-action shotguns in their hands.

Oliveira flashed his badge at one of the men, who glanced at Luiz.

'Who's your masked friend?'

'Informer. He's helping me out on a case.'

The guard shrugged. 'Whatever. You know the drill. Inside there, you're on your own. Get into trouble, don't expect us to come rushing in to save you.'

'You're all heart,' Oliveira replied sarcastically. He turned to Luiz. 'Stay close to me, OK?'

Pushing through the doors, they walked straight into hell.

The first thing that hit Luiz was the stench, a stomach-churning mix of sweat, excrement and burning electricity so strong he could almost taste it. He had to fight the urge to vomit. Looking around the hall, he saw that Polinter was filled with rows of metal cages. Jammed with ten times the number of people they were designed for, the cages were so overcrowded that the inmates were forced to stand up, their limbs spilling out through the bars. There were so many bodies in such a small space that there didn't seem to be enough oxygen in the air. Sweat dripped from the ceiling like rain. The floor beneath Luiz's feet was slippery with murky liquid and the walls were smeared with brown stains.

Luiz frowned. 'I can't see any guards. Where are they?'

'They don't usually come this far into the prison,' replied Oliveira, warily scanning the room. 'The only law that exists in this place is survival of the fittest.'

As he surveyed the cages, Luiz thought of the Comando Negro. Maybe Angel could survive in here, but Joker?

Livio? Imagining the friendly MC in this hellhole, he shuddered, instinctively drawing closer to Oliveira's side.

The policeman walked grimly past the cells, his jaw set and his hand resting on the handle of his gun. There were no cots inside the cages, merely hammocks fashioned from items of clothing. At the sight of the two newcomers, the prisoners reached out through the bars, their arms dangling imploringly towards them. Luiz couldn't look them in the eye. Instead he glanced at the rows of plastic bags and bottles hanging down the outside of the cage bars. He nudged Oliveira.

'What are they for?'

'The bags are filled with shit, the bottles with piss,' the policeman replied. 'There aren't any toilets here and the maids don't come round very often.'

Luiz made a face. 'Ugh. That's gross.'

'Tell me about it. Listen, while we're on the subject of hygiene – whatever you do, don't look up at the ceiling. The place is so filthy that the drips will give you eye infections. There're so many diseases in this place you'll probably get the plague.' He glanced at Luiz. 'Still glad you came with me?'

'No,' Luiz replied truthfully. 'But I'm here now. Where's the informer?'

Oliveira pointed down the corridor. 'The Comando Negro cells are this way.'

Although Luiz was slowly becoming accustomed to the dreadful smell, the humid atmosphere inside Polinter was making him feel dizzy. Sweat was pouring down his back, soaking his shirt. As he followed Oliveira through the prison, Luiz was surprised to hear the sound of voices singing. Turning a corner, he looked on with astonishment at the scene before him.

A church choir was standing on top of a makeshift stage, women in long, bright blue robes who clapped their hands together as they raised their voices to the heavens. At the front of the stage, a man in a suit was preaching into a microphone about God and redemption. A group of prisoners had been allowed out of their cages and were listening raptly as the man spoke, waving their hands in the air and cheering in agreement.

'What the hell's this?' Luiz whispered.

'Evangelicals,' replied Oliveira. 'They visit the prison from time to time, trying to convert the inmates to Christianity. There're plenty of sinners to save here. They sing, they pray, they exorcize the prisoners' demons. Come on – this isn't a sightseeing tour.'

As they moved away, the preacher with the microphone stepped into the audience of inmates and touched one of them on the forehead, chanting in a strange tongue Luiz couldn't understand. The prisoner collapsed to the ground and began writhing around as though he was on fire. The inmates around him roared their approval as the choir sang on and the preacher continued to speak in tongues.

Then, above the sound of the choir, Luiz heard a blood-curdling scream. It had come from one of the cells at the far end of the hall.

'Shit!' Oliveira swore, pulling a pistol from his belt.

The policeman broke into a run as another scream rent the air, before abruptly ceasing. Polinter was alive with noise now, the prisoners bouncing up and down in their cages like monkeys, hollering and whooping. As Luiz raced after Oliveira, the choir responded to the noise by breaking into a chorus at the top of their lungs. The inmate being exorcized was now foaming at the mouth, his limbs thrashing so violently that other prisoners were trying to pin him down.

Oliveira had stopped at a cell at the end of the corridor and was leaning on the bars as he peered inside. Catching up with the policeman, Luiz saw that the inmates beyond had pressed themselves against one side of the cage, revealing a body lying sprawled on the floor.

'Don't look, Luiz,' Juan said softly.

Too late.

The informer wasn't old – possibly the same age as Luiz. His fists were still bunched up in a defensive posture. Blood was pouring out from a stab wound in his left-hand side and his eyes were lifeless. But worst of all, someone had taken a knife to the corpse's back, tearing off flaps of skin to reveal a bloodied message to anyone with enough stomach to make out the two letters.

A 'C' and an 'N'. The initials of the Comando Negro.

19. Old Friends

Dazed, Luiz allowed Oliveira to lead him out of the prison's hellish labyrinth and into the late-afternoon fresh air. In the car park, he tore off his balaclava and was suddenly and violently sick. The policeman waited until Luiz's stomach was emptied, then wordlessly handed him a tissue.

'Sorry,' Luiz muttered, wiping his mouth. 'Wasn't prepared for that.' He retched again.

'Nothing to apologize for,' Oliveira said calmly. 'I'm sorry you had to see it. If we had got there five minutes earlier, maybe we could have stopped it.'

'Who do you think did it? It had to be one of the guys in the cage with him.'

Oliveira shrugged. 'Doubt we'll ever know for sure. All the guys in the cage were Comando Negro and you saw what happens to gang members who talk to the police. As soon as they found out the guy was an informer, he was a dead man walking. No one's going to tell us who stabbed him.'

'Do you think he really did know who the Doctor is?' asked Luiz.

'Doesn't matter either way now,' replied the policeman.

'That's between him and God. Listen, I've got to go back to the station. You want a lift anywhere?'

Luiz shook his head. 'I still feel pretty sick. I'm going to walk back to Santa Marta.'

'OK, then.' Oliveira patted him on the shoulder. 'Take care of yourself, Luiz. Don't do anything I wouldn't.'

The policeman climbed into his car and drove away. As the vehicle exited the prison car park, Luiz had an irrational urge to call Oliveira back. He kept silent, however, standing alone in the prison car park as the shadows began to lengthen around him.

Luiz trudged through the streets of the Zona Sul, not caring which direction he was going. Dusk had fallen over Rio and the city was beginning to come alive with people looking to party through the night. The streets were lit up with neon signs and flashing lights, thumping beats emanating from the bars and nightclubs. Somewhere a live samba band was playing, the drummer beating out a hypnotic rhythm.

Walking past the rows of souvenir shops and fast-food restaurants, Luiz passed a skinny young girl walking hand in hand with a sweaty American man old enough to be her grandfather. Luiz had lived in Rio long enough to recognize a sex tourist when he saw one. Whenever they started pawing at under-age girls in the middle of the street he had to fight the urge to punch them. The foreign tourists always talked about how exotic and exciting Rio was, but they never seemed to mention the children on the street

158

corners and in the saunas, selling their bodies for whatever they could get. In this city – where most of the girls were skinny not because they were dieting, but because they didn't have enough to eat – the glamour was only skin-deep.

Down at the beach, queues were forming by the volleyball courts as kids lined up to play *futevolei*. On the courts themselves, the players were heading and volleying the ball back and forth across the net, the ball never threatening to touch the ground. Briefly, Luiz wondered whether Gui would be among them, laughing and joking with their other friends, chatting up the girls as they walked past.

Amid all the hustle and bustle, Luiz felt lost and alone. He couldn't get the memory of the corpse's blank eyes out of his mind, nor the gaping wounds hacked into his flesh. *That's what happens to gang members who talk to the police*, Oliveira had told him. If that was the case, what would happen to Luiz if he was unmasked? Would someone find him lying face-down in the mud, letters carved into his back?

His mobile phone began vibrating in his shorts' pocket. Glancing down at the caller ID, Luiz saw that it was his foster parents. He was about to answer, when he suddenly put the phone away. The way Luiz felt right now, he would probably break down if he heard the sound of his mum's or his dad's voice. Then they wouldn't stop until they'd got the truth out of him, and it would all be for nothing. After all, it probably wouldn't be long now before they came home . . .

Luiz stopped in his tracks, people jostling his shoulders

like waves around an iceberg. With everything that was going on, he had completely lost track of what day it was. He had been back in the *favela* for nearly a week now. It was Tuesday – and his parents were supposed to be coming back on Friday. That meant he had only three days left to uncover the identity of the Doctor and get Ana out of jail. Three days? It seemed impossible.

Luiz walked on, his steps taking him away from the centre of the Zona Sul and into the quiet backstreets that led back to Santa Marta. It was no use feeling sorry for himself, he thought sternly. Self-pity wasn't going to set Ana free. He decided that he would try to talk to Angel that night. Perhaps if he mentioned Councillor Cruz, the *dono* might let something slip, especially if the two of them had just met in the Casa Bahia. Trojan had been right from the start – Angel was the key to everything. Now that he had finally accepted Luiz as a member of the Comando Negro, perhaps he would be more open around him.

With a plan forming in his head, Luiz strode along with renewed vigour. He cut down a narrow alleyway, the Santa Marta hillside suddenly emerging out of the night above his head. The exuberant noise of the Zona Sul had faded away into the background. Somewhere close by, a police siren wailed. Ahead of him a mangy dog was pawing through an overturned dustbin. Its head snapped up at the sound of Luiz approaching – with a yelp, it scuttled away.

Luiz was in the darkest depths of the alleyway when he heard a noise behind him.

'Luiz!' a voice called out, in a mocking, childlike tone. 'I can see you!'

Luiz whirled round. 'Who's there?'

There was a movement in the alleyway shadows; a shock of bleached-blond hair in the darkness.

It was Stripe.

The chief *soldado* of the Comando Negro swaggered towards him, a faint smile on his face. His eyes – never clear at the best of times – were bleary, his pupils dilated. As he looked at Luiz, Stripe frowned, as though he was having difficulty focusing. He had clearly been snorting line after line of coke. In his trembling hands, he was carrying his beloved AK-47 assault rifle. The safety catch was off.

'Stripe!' said Luiz, desperate to sound friendly. 'What are you doing here?'

The boy waved his hand around vaguely. 'You know,' he said. 'What about you?'

'I . . . went shopping downtown,' Luiz stammered. 'Wanted to get some clothes and shit like that.'

Stripe tapped his finger thoughtfully against his cheek. 'Didn't do so well, did you?'

'What?'

'Your hands are empty,' said Stripe, gesturing at him with his gun. 'Guess you didn't buy anything.'

'Oh, er, no,' Luiz said hastily. 'Couldn't find anything I liked the look of.' He tried to change the subject. 'I haven't seen you for ages. What have you been up to?'

Stripe sniffed, pinching the end of his nose. 'Following you.'

Luiz's blood froze. 'What do you mean?'

'I *mean*,' Stripe said deliberately, 'that ever since that argument with Angel, I've been keeping an eye on you. And you've been a busy boy today, haven't you? First of all you spy on Angel, then you go to Polinter with that new buddy of yours.' He chuckled. 'You know, it's funny, but the way that guy flashed his badge at the prison guards, I could have sworn he was a cop. But then, you're in the Comando Negro, aren't you, Luiz? And no gang member would ever hang out with a cop, would they?'

'I don't know what you're talking about,' Luiz said weakly, backing up against a wire fence. 'Angel's right – you do too much coke. It's making you crazy.'

Stripe leaned forward. 'Crazy?' he hissed. 'Me? I knew you were bullshitting from day one. That's why I tried to take care of you during the initiation. But Livio, Joker, even Angel, man, they all fell for it. They're the crazy ones, Luiz, not me. And now I'm going to do what they should have done a week ago.'

As Stripe levelled his gun, Luiz leaped at him, fists swinging. Catching the boy with a glancing blow on the side of the head, he knocked the gun from Stripe's hands, sending it skittering down the alleyway. Stripe responded by headbutting Luiz in the temple. He was smiling, as though delighted by the opportunity to cause him pain.

For a couple of minutes the two boys wrestled with one another, grappling with headlocks as though they were having a playground scuffle. Luiz was strong and quick, but Stripe had been killing people for years. When Luiz dropped to the floor to deliver a sweeping kick, the *soldado* saw it coming. Hurdling the leg, he volleyed Luiz viciously in the groin. Luiz screamed in agony, stars of pain exploding in front of his eyes. Stripe kicked him again, in the head this time, forcing Luiz to curl up in a defensive bundle.

As kicks rained down upon his body, Luiz clutched at his neck, blindly searching for the crucifix with the distress button, only to discover it was no longer hanging there. It must have been ripped off in the struggle. Even if they could have got here in time, no one from Trojan was going to be coming to save him.

Stripe had stopped kicking him and had retrieved his AK-47 from the other side of the alleyway. He stood over the bleeding figure of Luiz, a manic grin plastered across his face.

'Don't shoot,' Luiz breathed. 'Please.'

Stripe laughed harshly.

'You know, sometimes I gotta put a cap in someone and it's just business.' He spat at Luiz, then trained his assault rifle at his forehead. 'This one's going to be pure pleasure.'

Luiz closed his eyes, as the sound of a gunshot exploded in his ears.

20. Turf Wars

He wasn't dead.

Opening his eyes, Luiz saw that Stripe was still standing over him. There was a shocked expression on the boy's face. His black T-shirt was stained with blood. Looking beyond Stripe, Luiz saw that there was another boy standing in the gloom behind him. As Stripe turned slowly round, the boy fired again. Stripe flinched, as though he had been stung. Another shot rang out, hitting Stripe in the face this time. The Comando Negro's chief soldier collapsed to the floor, his face a broken red mess.

Luiz was too shocked to move. He lay there, covered in a mixture of Stripe's blood and his own, as Dog stepped into the light and walked calmly over to him. The boy was holding a shotgun, which looked huge in his small hands. As he approached Stripe's body, Dog fired another bullet into the corpse.

'Bastard,' he said, poking it with his toe. 'Not so tough now, are you?' He looked across at Luiz. 'You OK?'

'You saved me,' Luiz croaked.

'I guess. I owed you after what happened during the game anyway. No one else was going to step in. Stripe would have killed me. After that, I knew I was going to have to kill him.'

'What's Angel going to say? Stripe may have been a bastard, but he was Comando Negro.'

Dog shrugged. 'Screw Angel. Screw them all. It was me who told the Quarto Comando about the deal at the hotel. I overheard Angel telling Joker about it.'

'You?' gasped Luiz. 'But why?'

'I had to tell them something to make them trust me. I'm joining the Quarto Comando.'

'You're leaving the Comando Negro?'

Dog nodded. 'I'm sick of getting treated like a baby. Stripe was the worst, but none of you thought I could become a *soldado*. Now you'll see.'

'But you can't just change gangs!'

'Angel did, didn't he? I'm going to be as big as him. You tell Angel, he comes for me and he'll end up just like Stripe. He's not the only one with a shotgun now. Pass it on.'

Luiz nodded slowly.

'Good,' Dog said confidently. 'I always liked you. You're not like the rest of them. See you, Luiz.'

As he made to leave, Dog noticed something on the floor of the alleyway. He bent down and picked it up.

'This yours?' he said. He held up the gleaming crucifix.

Luiz nodded. Dog tossed it over to him.

'You're going to need it. Can't rely on me to save your ass any more. We're even now, Luiz. You'd better hope you don't see me again.'

As he watched the little boy walk away into the night, Luiz

was suddenly less certain that Dog was going to spend the rest of his life as a whipping boy. Struggling to his feet, he began limping back in the direction of Santa Marta, leaving Stripe's body in a pool of blood in the alleyway.

'What the hell happened to you?'

Livio stared open-mouthed as Luiz walked wearily up the steps to his shack, his face caked with dried blood. The MC, with his feet up, was drinking and smoking while he listened to some *baile-funk* tunes belting out from a battered CD player.

'I had a rough day,' Luiz said drily. 'Where's Angel? I need to talk to him.'

Livio drained his beer and led Luiz across Santa Marta to Angel's shack. The *dono* listened quietly as Luiz told him what had happened – careful to omit the fact that Stripe had been following him around all day. When he heard about Stripe's death, Angel looked astonished; when he heard about Dog's defection to the Quarto Comando, the *dono* exploded.

'The little shit!' he shouted. 'I'm going to kill him! Him and his new gang!'

'Right now?' Livio said dubiously.

Angel flashed him a dangerous look. 'What's wrong, MC – not got the stomach for it?'

'Hey, I run with you, you know that! It's just that we're taking on the Compadres, we're taking on Quarto Comando, we've still got the cops sniffing round our asses, and we've just lost one of our best *soldados*. I don't how much more we can take on, *dono*.'

Angel eyeballed Livio coldly.

'This is what we do,' he snarled. 'We fight, we kill, we die. We are the Comando Negro – we don't show any weakness. There is no end. There is no way out. You understand me?'

As Livio nodded, the rage in Angel's eyes dimmed.

'We gotta stay together, Livio,' he said softly. 'You and me, Joker, Luiz. We're all brothers, man.' He glanced at Luiz. 'Right?'

'Right,' Luiz agreed, feeling sick even as he did so.

The *dono* picked up his Remington. 'Grab some beers from the fridge and come with me,' he ordered.

'Where are we going?' asked Livio.

Angel smiled.

'First, we're going to find my brother and drag him away from whichever girl he's annoying now. Then we're getting reinforcements.'

Two hours later and Angel halted a pickup truck outside a warehouse in a quiet district to the east of Rio. He carefully scanned the area before getting out from the vehicle.

'Keep your eyes peeled,' he said crisply. 'I phoned ahead so we're expected, but if you see anything moving I want to know about it.'

The *dono* seemed even more watchful than ever. Luiz wondered where they were, whether or not they were trespassing in another gang's territory. As they moved warily towards the warehouse door, he saw that someone had drawn a bullet on the wall in blue spray-paint. Underneath the bullet were the words Comando Azul. Luiz tapped Joker on the arm.

'Comando Azul? Which gang is that? I've never heard of them.'

Joker snorted. 'They usually go by another name. Cops.'

Luiz stared at the graffiti tag in astonishment. The police had marked their territory – just like the gangs they fought against.

'Don't know why you're looking so surprised,' Joker said. 'Everyone knows all the cops in Rio are bent. My brother once told me that, when he ran with the Compadres, their *dono* was kidnapped by the police and held for ransom. It cost them thousands to get him back. Jesus, Luiz, if they weren't crooked, why the hell would they be here?'

Angel rapped on the metal door. It opened a crack, revealing a middle-aged man with a tanned skin and a thick moustache. He was dressed in a police uniform.

'You Angel?' he said.

'Yeah,' the *dono* replied. 'The Doctor spoke to you?'

The policeman nodded, then gestured for the Comando Negro to enter the warehouse. Luiz brought up the rear, unsure of what lay in store inside. The answer, he discovered as he walked into the dimly lit space, could be summed up in one word.

Guns.

Everywhere he looked, there were guns. Handguns, assault rifles, shotguns, stacked up against the walls and the shelves, reaching all the way up to the ceiling. Some had simply been tossed on top of one another, creating giant metal pyres of firearms. From gleaming new machine-guns to what looked like antique pistols, there had to be tens of thousands of weapons here.

'You picked a good time to come and see us,' the police-man said, in a conversational tone of voice. 'We raided an Angolan ship off the coast the other day and found a small arsenal on board. Hand grenades, bombs, landmines – some real heavy-duty shit. Help yourself.'

Immediately the Comando Negro scattered among the aisles, diving into piles of guns as though they were kids in a toyshop. As he followed them around, Luiz couldn't help but think of Juan Oliveira. The *favela*-dwelling cop seemed such a good guy. What would he say if he could see this? Did he know cops who sold gangs guns? Did he do it too?

'Holy shit!'

He looked up to see Livio balancing a rocket launcher on his shoulder.

'Put that down, Livio,' Angel shouted from across the warehouse. 'You're making me nervous just touching that thing.'

Reluctantly, the MC put the rocket launcher back. As the gang went about selecting their weapons, the police-man saw Luiz eyeing a row of pistols. He picked up a small handgun and passed it to him.

'Check this one out. It's a Sig Sauer 226. German-manufactured, so you know it's going to be a reliable piece.'

The cop smiled encouragingly, as though he was selling shoes or sweets.

Luiz looked down the sight and checked the balance of the weapon.

'Seems OK,' he said, unsure of how to respond. 'I'll take it.'

Luiz stuck the Sig Sauer into the waistband of his shorts with a heavy heart. Finally, he had a gun, and it was looking more likely with each second that he was going to have to use it.

'This is the greatest place ever!' Joker called out. He was carrying an assault rifle in each hand, his face wreathed in a broad smile. 'No one's going to mess with us now!'

'That's not what I've heard,' the policeman replied.

Angel looked up sharply.

'What do you mean?'

'That windbag Cruz from the council has finally persuaded the police chiefs that your little gang needs putting out of business. Expect a visit from CORE soon.'

The temperature in the warehouse seemed to drop a couple of degrees. Even if Luiz hadn't heard of CORE – Rio's elite police SWAT unit – the sudden pensive looks on the faces of the Comando Negro would have told him all he needed to know.

Angel spat on the floor, breaking the grim silence.

'Thanks for the warning.' The *dono* tossed the policeman two wads of notes bound together with elastic bands.

'Hey, all part of the service,' the man replied, counting through the notes. 'Come round whenever you feel like it.'

Luiz waited until they had left the warehouse and were

crossing the concrete back to the pickup truck before grabbing Livio.

'CORE are coming? That means trouble, right?'

The MC's face was grim.

'You have no idea,' he said.

21. Cruz Control

In the centre of Rio, Cinelândia square was the bustling heartbeat of the city's urban life. Removed from the beaches of Copacabana and Ipanema – and the sun-worshippers who lazed upon their sands – here the streets were thronged with businessmen and professionals. The towering skyscrapers obscured everything but the distinctive hump of *Pão de Açúcar* – Sugarloaf Mountain. From the middle of Cinelândia square, grand buildings were visible in every direction: the Municipal Theatre, the Brazilian National Library – and the council meeting hall.

Given the number of rallies and demonstrations that took place in the square, on any particular day it wasn't unusual to see politicians making public speeches there. That morning, Councillor Jorge Cruz had taken up a position on the steps of the council hall and was in the middle of a thunderous denunciation of the *favela* gangs. At the back of the massed ranks of bored reporters and casual bystanders, a teenage boy was watching Cruz speak. Luiz had been waiting in the square for this moment since dawn, his heart pounding and the gun's cold metal pressing against his skin with a horrible insistence.

After the Comando Negro's jubilation inside the police warehouse, the policeman's parting warning had dampened the mood on the journey home. As Angel drove the pickup truck silently back to Santa Marta, Livio leaned over towards Luiz and asked in a low whisper, 'Have you seen CORE raid a *favela* before?'

Luiz shook his head.

'Count yourself lucky. They're mean bastards. They come in all guns blazing and they shoot to kill.'

'Double the lookouts at the *boca*,' Angel said from the driver's seat. 'We'll see them coming. If they want a fire-fight, they'll get one. They don't know Santa Marta like we do.'

But for all the *dono*'s defiant words, there was an undercurrent of uncertainty in Angel's voice. What with the Compadres, Quarto Comando and now CORE circling around Santa Marta, it was impossible to escape the feeling of a trap closing around them. It was at that moment that Luiz had realized what he had to do. He had to find the Doctor before the Comando Negro came under attack – which meant he had to find Councillor Jorge Cruz.

The next morning he had risen before the sun, slipping out past the *boca* and down into the city. He headed straight for Cinelândia – an area his parents had spent a great deal of time in, especially during their own investigations into Councillor Cruz. Now Luiz was following in their footsteps, only he was armed. If he had to threaten Cruz to get the truth out of him, then he would do so.

The crowd burst into applause as Cruz's speech came to

its resounding conclusion. The councillor waved, before moving back towards the council hall's entrance. Making to go after him, Luiz was suddenly aware of a hand on his arm.

'Excuse me, son?'

A man was looking down at him. Although he was dressed casually, an earpiece wire was curling down the back of his neck and his free hand was resting on a bulky shape inside his jacket.

'Sorry,' Luiz muttered hurriedly. 'Gotta run.'

The man didn't let go. He smiled. 'What's the rush?'

Luiz made to break away.

'Look out – he's armed!' a voice cried out.

A woman next to Luiz screamed loudly and turned to flee. Before he could follow suit, a burly arm snaked around Luiz's neck, grabbing it in a sleeper hold. Caught off guard, Luiz flailed his arms in an attempt to free himself, but the man's grip was as tight as a vice. Black spots began to appear in front of Luiz's eyes. The last thing he saw before he passed out was a scrum of men descending upon him.

When he came to, he found himself lying down in a cramped space, his knees tucked up underneath his chin. There was a blindfold over his eyes and his hands were cuffed behind his back. His gun was gone. A loud sound was growling very close to his head – groggily, Luiz realized it was an engine. He was in the boot of a car. Trapped, there was nothing he could do but wait, and try to fight the tide of panic rising within him.

After about half an hour, the car slowed. He heard the sound of an electronic beeping and then the car purred up a gravel driveway. As the boot was popped open, strong hands hauled Luiz to his feet. Still blindfolded, he was pushed along the driveway, his feet crunching on the gravel. Luiz heard a latch click open and his feet felt smooth paving stones beneath them. Somewhere in the distance, waves were crashing against the shoreline.

Luiz was pushed abruptly down into a seat, his hands still cuffed impotently behind his back. The blindfold was torn from his eyes, exposing a world of piercing bright sunlight. He looked around, blinking.

He was sitting at a poolside table at the rear of a luxurious, two-storey villa. Over his shoulder, a deserted strip of beach ran down to the foaming breakers at the water's edge. Luiz didn't recognize the coastline, couldn't even be sure whether he was still in Rio. He was aware that a man was standing behind him: the bodyguard with the earpiece from the square. On the other side of the pool, a woman in a tiny blue bikini was stretched out on a towel, tinny music blaring from her headphones. But it was the person sitting opposite Luiz who grabbed his attention.

Across the table, Councillor Jorge Cruz was hungrily attacking a plate of pork ribs, his mouth ringed with sauce. Having changed out of his suit, he was now clad in a pair of khaki shorts and a Lacoste polo shirt, which was stained with sweat not only under the armpits but also beneath a sizeable pair of man-breasts. Cruz ate noisily, tearing the meat from the bone with his teeth like a dog. With a sinking heart, Luiz saw that his Sig Sauer 226 was lying on the table next to the councillor.

Luiz sat in silence until the councillor pushed his plate away, finally sated. Cruz took a deep gulp from a glass of cold beer and then asked casually, 'So who sent you?'

'What?' said Luiz, confused.

The councillor made a signal and Luiz received a ringing blow to the back of the head from the bodyguard behind him. He rocked forward in his seat, feeling nauseous from the pain. Cruz gave him a hard look.

'We'll try that again. Who sent you?'

'No one sent me, I swear!' Luiz shouted. 'I don't know what you're talking about!'

Cruz sighed and nodded again at his bodyguard. Another thundering blow landed on the back of Luiz's head. Thankfully, he was still feeling numb from the first blow, though even that fact couldn't entirely deaden the sting.

'Carlos can do this all day, you know,' Cruz continued. 'He doesn't tire easily.'

'But I'm telling you the truth!' Luiz protested.

Cruz shook his head. 'You kids. You're all as dumb as each other. Do you know how many death threats I've received? Did you think you could just turn up to one of my speeches with a gun stuffed into your shorts and no one would notice?' He pointedly tapped Luiz's Sig Sauer. 'Didn't you realize that my men are always looking out for little sewer rats like you who want to take potshots at me?'

Seeing the stubborn look on Luiz's face, Cruz glanced up at his bodyguard.

'I think you can remove the handcuffs, Carlos. If the little rat tries anything, shoot him in the back of the head.'

The man behind Luiz reached down and brusquely unlocked the handcuffs. With his hands freed, Luiz gingerly massaged the back of his head and neck, surreptitiously taking hold of his GPS crucifix and pressing the ends of the horizontal beam together. Richard Madison had always sworn that Trojan could track down the distress signal no matter where it was sent from. Luiz offered up a silent prayer that the Brit had been telling the truth.

'You can't hurt me,' he said, trying to sound braver than he felt. 'As soon as you turn me over to the police I'm going to tell them all about you.'

'Really?' Cruz raised a bushy eyebrow. 'And what *exactly* are you going to say?'

'I'll tell them I know exactly who you are!' Luiz blurted out. 'You're the Doctor!'

Cruz paused for a second, then burst into laughter.

'*I'm* the Doctor? You stupid kid!'

'Don't try and deny it,' Luiz said fiercely. 'You met Angel in the Casa Bahia – I saw you!'

Cruz wiped his sticky fingers on a napkin before tossing it to one side. 'You might well have seen me in the Casa Bahia, but I wasn't meeting that hoodlum.'

'But you know who Angel is.'

'I make it my business to know all about the Comando Negro. I'd be the last person who'd deal with them, though. At this rate, they're going to screw up everything.'

Luiz rubbed the back of his head again, a suspicious look on his face. 'What do you mean?'

'For years I've had a certain . . . vested interest in Santa Marta,' Cruz said. 'One that doesn't fit in very well with scum like you running around pushing drugs and killing each other.'

'What sort of interest?'

'Over time I've managed to acquire some land in that particular *favela* for a very reasonable rate.'

Luiz thought back to his parents' investigations into Cruz; their suspicions of dodgy land deals. Slowly things began to fall into place.

'That's why you hate the Comando Negro! You want the *favela* for yourself!'

'Smart kid. Right now the land I own is worthless. But if the police take out the Comando Negro, maybe raze the *favela* to the ground while they're at it, then I can start to transform Santa Marta. In a few years' time, I'll be selling luxury apartments boasting the best views of Rio. It'll be like sitting on a goldmine.'

Luiz's head spun as he tried to take it all in. 'But then, if you're not the Doctor – who is?'

The councillor chuckled, sitting back in his seat. 'You really don't get it, do you?' He leaned forward. 'Angel's the Doctor.'

'That's impossible!' Luiz protested. 'I heard Angel talking to the Doctor on the phone!'

'Really? You heard the Doctor's voice?'

Luiz faltered. 'No, but . . . he didn't know I was there!'

Cruz chuckled thickly. 'Or at least that's what he wanted you to think. Mouthy kid like you, that would be perfect. I've got to hand it to Angel – he ain't so dumb for a *favela* kid. He should forget all this gang bullshit and go into politics.'

Luiz sat stunned. He had been so sure that there was a Doctor – it couldn't be Angel. Could it?

'Why?' he said finally.

'All these gangs are looking for an edge over one another. What better than some kind of super-villain with money, power and knowledge? Not just another snot-nosed *favela* thug?'

'I don't care what you say,' Luiz blustered. 'Even if you're not the Doctor, you're still a crook. I'm going to make sure everyone finds out what you're up to.'

Cruz laughed. 'And what makes you think you're going to live long enough to tell anyone anything?'

'You can't kill me!'

'I'm a powerful and respected local figure. You're a piece of shit from the *favelas*. You really think I'm going to let you get in the way?' Cruz rose to his feet. 'Carlos, could you take care of our little friend here please?'

Before Luiz could react, there was a movement from inside the villa. A glass door slid open and a woman stepped smoothly down on to the patio.

It was Valerie Singer.

22. Special Delivery

Jorge Cruz stared dumbly at the Israeli woman.

'Who the hell are you? And how did you get into my house?'

'I asked nicely,' Valerie replied. 'And my name isn't important right now.'

'Whoever you are, lady,' Carlos said menacingly from behind Luiz, 'you're trespassing on private property. I'd suggest you leave now.'

'Yeah, your friends inside said the same thing,' Valerie said, unruffled. 'I politely disagreed.'

'Where are my men?' asked Cruz, his eyes narrowing.

By way of reply, Valerie moved away from the patio door. Inside the house, Luiz caught a glimpse of a man's leg stretched out across the floor.

'Carlos!' Cruz shouted.

The bodyguard didn't have time to blink. In one lightning-quick motion, Valerie pulled out a pistol with a silencer fixed to the barrel and fired over Luiz's head. There was a muted *pfft* as the gun went off and a horrible sound of metal impacting on bone. Luiz turned round to see Carlos topple to the floor, a bloodied hole in his forehead.

Valerie walked towards the table, her gun trained steadily on Cruz. There was the thinnest of smiles on her face. The councillor had turned pale, his eyes flicking left and right as he looked for an escape route.

'Don't bother calling for help,' Valerie warned him. 'There's no one left to rescue you. Unless she's going to do it.'

She nodded at the woman in the blue bikini sunbathing on the other side of the pool. To Luiz's amazement, he saw that the woman hadn't moved. Her eyes were still shut, the blaring music in her earphones keeping her blissfully unaware of the gunshot.

'That's my wife,' Cruz said, between clenched teeth. 'Keep her out of this.'

Valerie glanced scornfully over at the woman. 'A little young for you, isn't she, Jorge?'

'What do you want?' Cruz asked sharply.

'The boy.'

'*Him?* What do you want with him?'

'That's my business.'

As Valerie gestured at Luiz to move over to her, he slowly got to his feet, retrieving his Sig Sauer from the table as he went past. The councillor glared at him balefully.

'We're leaving now,' said Valerie. 'I wouldn't advise you to try to follow us.'

Cruz's face had turned mottled with rage.

'This is my city – you can't hide from me!' he shouted. 'Wherever you go, I'll find you!'

Valerie laughed icily. 'I very much doubt it. But look how easily I found you. Be grateful that you're still breathing. Your lovely wife too.'

As they backed away into the villa, the councillor stood up in his seat, shaking with rage.

'This isn't over, you hear me!' he bellowed. 'You and all your little buddies are finished! CORE's heading out to Santa Marta as we speak. By the time they've finished with the Comando Negro, you won't be able to tell which corpse is which!'

Numbed by Cruz's words, Luiz allowed Valerie to lead him through the villa, past the corpse of another of the councillor's bodyguards. Glancing down the hallway, Luiz saw the bodies of two more men slumped lifelessly against the wall.

'You killed all these men?' he gasped.

'Don't be impressed,' Valerie replied, stepping disdainfully over the bodies. 'They were amateurs.'

Leaving the villa through the open front door, they hurried along the gravel driveway. Beyond the ornate front gates, a car was waiting for them – the white Mercedes with the tinted windows that had first taken Luiz to Trojan's warehouse.

'You came alone?' Luiz asked Valerie, surprised.

'Me and the driver.' She gave him a sideways glance. 'Was I not enough?'

'It's not that. It's just . . . I'm surprised you were the one who came, that's all.'

'I was the agent on call,' Valerie said coldly, as she

opened the back-seat door. 'Don't think that I'm getting sentimental.'

'Fat chance of that,' Luiz muttered, climbing inside the car.

They had barely closed the door before the unseen driver gunned the engine. The car sped away down the coastal road, leaving Councillor Cruz's villa shrouded in silence, the front door swinging forlornly in the breeze.

As the Mercedes hurtled back towards the centre of Rio, Valerie lit up another one of her foul-smelling cigarettes.

'So,' she began briskly, 'do you want to tell me how you ended up being held at gunpoint by one of Rio's most prominent assholes?'

Luiz looked down at his feet. 'Juan Oliveira and I saw Cruz at the Casa Bahia when Angel went there. I thought he was the Doctor, but I couldn't prove it.'

'So you were just going to go up to him and ask him?'

'I did ask him.'

Valerie laughed with surprise. 'I'll give you one thing, Luiz — you've got bottle. And what did our good council-lor say?'

'He's not the Doctor. He's trying to shut down the Comando Negro because he's bought land in Santa Marta. He wants to develop on it.'

Valerie shook her head, exhaling another thick cloud of smoke. 'This city.'

'That wasn't all he said.' Luiz paused. 'Cruz reckons that Angel is the Doctor.'

'Really?' The Israeli woman raised an eyebrow. 'And what do you think?'

'I don't know. It doesn't really make sense to me, but if it's not Cruz . . .'

'It won't matter any more. The mission's bound to be called off now.'

'What?'

'After what just happened with Cruz, there's no way we can keep sniffing around the Comando Negro. Didn't you see what happened back there, Luiz? I killed four of his bodyguards! He'll have men trawling the city for the pair of us as we speak.'

'But if the mission's over, what about Ana?'

'Who knows?' Valerie shrugged. 'Maybe Jordan will get her out anyway. He can be soft about this sort of thing. But if you ask me we won't have the time. Trojan will have to leave Rio as soon as possible.'

'And what about the Comando Negro? You heard what Cruz said. I've got to warn them about CORE!'

'You don't need to warn them about anything. You were sent in to Santa Marta to bring them down, remember?'

'I told you I'd find the Doctor,' Luiz said fiercely. 'Livio isn't the Doctor. He needs to know that CORE are coming for him now.'

Valerie sighed. 'Madison warned me you were getting attached to this gang. I didn't think you'd be so stupid.'

Looking out of the window, Luiz saw that the Mercedes had crossed the Zona Sul and was now passing through his old neighbourhood of Botafogo.

'Don't worry about me,' he said suddenly. 'Just let me out here.'

'I don't think so,' replied Valerie. 'We're going back to the warehouse now.'

'I said, let me out here.' Luiz was suddenly aware that the Sig Sauer 226 was in his hands and pointing straight at Valerie. It was almost as if he hadn't moved, and someone else was controlling him.

Valerie's eyes flicked to the gun. 'Your hand's trembling,' she said matter-of-factly.

Luiz didn't need to look down to know that she was telling the truth.

'Maybe, but do you think I'm going to miss from here? Trojan taught me how to fire a gun, remember? Let me out. Now!'

Valerie banged on the driver's partition.

'Stop the car,' she ordered curtly.

As the Mercedes drew up to the side of the road, Luiz opened the door behind him and backed out of the car, still shakily pointing his gun at Valerie. There wasn't a trace of emotion on her face.

'Once you walk away, that's it,' she said. 'If you get into trouble, you're on your own.' Her voice softened slightly. 'Are you really sure you want to do this?'

But Luiz was already running.

In truth, Luiz wasn't sure what he was doing any more. It felt as though everyone needed his help at the same time, pulling him in different directions. By trying to warn Livio,

Luiz knew he might be jeopardizing Ana's freedom. On the other hand, with his mission over and the heat on, he found it hard to believe that Trojan would risk further exposure by trying to get his sister out of jail. The only thing Luiz *was* sure about was the fact that he owed Livio big time and now the MC's life was in danger. If he didn't even try to warn his friend, how could he look himself in the mirror again?

Stuffing his gun into his waistband, Luiz raced through Botafogo to the bottom of Santa Marta and up the hill. He jogged past the *boca*, no longer troubled by the guards at the checkpoint, and through the streets of the *favela*. Whereas before the pounding of samba drums had provided the soundtrack to joyful celebrations, now to Luiz they sounded like the clock on a time bomb, inexorably counting down the seconds to destruction.

He found the command of the Comando Negro in the square outside Angel's shack. Two small pickup trucks packed with wooden crates were parked out in the dust and members of the gang were swarming over them, handing the crates down and carrying them away. Luiz saw Livio standing on the back of one of the trucks, puffing with exertion as he hoisted down a large crate. Seeing his friend, the MC stuck up his middle finger at him.

'Now you show up!' he shouted. 'I was looking for you all morning, you bastard! I've had to lift most of these crates on my own!'

Given the number of gang members around him, it didn't look as though that had been the case, but Luiz held up an apologetic hand anyway. On the steps of his house, he saw Angel was standing watch over the unloading, his arms folded. At the sight of Luiz, the *dono* beckoned him to one side. He glanced at Luiz's flushed cheeks.

'Been out for a run?'

'I had to pick up some things downtown,' Luiz lied. 'I heard at the *boca* that you needed a hand, so I got here as quick as I could.' He gestured towards the trucks. 'I'll go and give Livio a hand now.'

'You'll stand still and shut up.'

The ominous look in the *dono*'s eyes stopped Luiz in his tracks. Silently itching with impatience, Luiz waited as Angel subjected him to a searching gaze.

'While you were out messing around, we've been handling another delivery day,' the *dono* said eventually. 'You're no use to me outside the *favela*, Luiz. You know that shit we're in right now.'

'I'm really sorry, Angel, I didn't –'

Luiz was interrupted by a loud crash. Angel whirled round to see Livio standing on the edge of the truck, a crate lying in the dust below his feet. There was a sheepish look on the MC's face.

Angel stalked over to inspect the damaged crate. There was a jagged crack down one of the wooden sides, exposing the telltale white flash of cocaine packages.

'Livio,' the *dono* said, sighing, 'I swear to God that you are the clumsiest shit I have ever seen in my life.'

'If it had been a burger, he wouldn't have dropped it,' Joker called out.

'Hey!' said Livio, in an injured tone of voice. 'You're

just jealous because the girls can see your ribs sticking out.'

'I'm amazed you haven't poured barbecue sauce on them and tried to eat them,' Joker shot back.

'Leave it, Rafael,' barked Angel. 'You can shoot your mouth off *after* we've put these crates away.'

Joker was about to reply, but Angel held up his hand sharply for silence.

'Quiet!' he shouted.

Immediately the Comando Negro froze. In the silence, Luiz heard the distant sound of wheels rumbling up the hillside. His heart sank. He was too late.

'It's coming from the *boca*,' said Joker. 'What the hell is that?'

Angel flicked on his radio phone and quickly tapped a number into it. 'This is Angel. What's going on down there?'

There was a pause and then the radio phone crackled into life.

'It's CORE!' a voice shouted back. 'They're coming!'

Before the guard could say any more, there was a crackle of gunfire and the radio phone went dead.

23. Air Raid

As the gang members stared at one another in horror, it was the *dono* of the Comando Negro who swung into action.

'You!' Angel barked at a young *soldado*. 'Get these trucks out of here! Take them back to the warehouse downtown! If the cops get their hands on the drugs, I'm going to blame you, understand?'

The boy nodded, swallowing nervously.

'The rest of you, tool up and get down to the *boca*. These CORE bastards are going to regret the day they stepped foot inside Santa Marta. Now MOVE!'

As the square hurriedly emptied in a confusion of shouts and squealing tyres, Angel ran over to his shack and tossed his shotgun on to the low roof, hauling himself up after it. Livio and Joker were barely a step behind him, the MC's feet struggling for purchase on the wall before he finally managed to scramble on to the roof. Luiz took a wistful look at the alleyways leading out of the square and away to safety, then shook his head and followed them. Reaching for a handhold on the lip of the roof, he pulled himself up and swung his legs over the top.

From his vantage point on Angel's shack, Luiz could see all of Santa Marta sprawling out below him. Down at the *boca*, pandemonium reigned. Black armoured personnel carriers were grinding up the narrow road like giant metal beetles, as the sound of gunfire echoed around the *favela*. All of the vehicles were marked with CORE's insignia – a pair of crossed M16s and a skull with a knife through it. Members of the Comando Negro were huddled behind sandbags and in doorways, vainly trying to return fire. It was clear that, for once, they were hopelessly outgunned. Already some people were fleeing away across the rooftops, while Luiz could see several bodies lying prostrate in the road.

'Shit,' panted Livio, hands on his hips. 'They aren't going to last a second.'

'Not if we don't help them,' Angel replied, his eyes gleaming. 'We need to get down there.'

'You sure about that, bro?' asked Joker. 'Taking on the Compadres is one thing, but this is CORE!'

The *dono* whirled round and grabbed Joker by the throat.

'Come with me to the *boca* or I'll shoot you right now,' said Angel in a deathly whisper. 'Family or not.'

The two brothers stood staring at each other, Joker's face etched with shock. Despite everything he knew about Angel, Luiz had never thought that he would threaten his own blood.

For a few seconds no one moved. No one even breathed.

'Er, Angel . . .?' Livio said uncertainly.

The MC was looking up at the hillside behind them, shielding his eyes as he squinted into the sun.

'What is it?' snapped Angel.

'We've got trouble.'

Luiz followed the MC's gaze. At first glance, everything looked normal. Then, above the sounds of battle raging at the *boca*, he heard a low scudding noise coming from beyond the summit of Santa Marta. Peering into the sunshine, Luiz saw a dark silhouette rise up over the crest of the hill. A helicopter. Hovering in the air, it dipped its nose and flew forward – straight towards the shack.

'Take cover!' Angel shouted.

As the helicopter buzzed in overhead, the Comando Negro scattered. Luiz sprinted across the roof and dived off the edge, bullets exploding into the roof where he had been standing. He landed awkwardly, his ankle turning on the hard ground. Gritting his teeth through the pain, he pressed himself against the wall of Angel's shack as the helicopter thundered over him, then banked for another pass.

Hobbling over to an open window, Luiz clambered inside, where he found Livio squatting on his haunches, loading an assault rifle.

'One of Angel's,' the MC shouted above the din. 'Let's see how they like this! You OK?'

Luiz nodded, trying to ignore the throbbing pain in his ankle.

The shack was shrouded in shadow as the helicopter took another pass, flying so low that the flimsy building reverberated to the whirring of its rotors. Livio raced over to the window and fired a stream of bullets up into the air, spraying spent cartridges across the floor.

Passing unscathed over the top of the building, the helicopter hovered metres above the square in front of Angel's shack, whipping up a blinding storm of dust. The noise was deafening. As Luiz looked on, two lengths of cable dropped down from the helicopter and two commandos slid down them to the ground. They were dressed in all black, their faces masked by balaclavas. Instantly they were on their feet, M4 assault rifles trained on the shack.

Luiz froze. He was dimly aware that Livio was by his side again, hurriedly reloading his assault rifle. Something important was nagging at him at the back of his mind, but with all the noise and the chaos it was difficult to think. As the commandos crept towards the shack, Luiz moved back against the wall, which was still trembling from the vibrations of the helicopter's blades.

That was it. The wall. Suddenly Luiz remembered Livio breaking off chunks of masonry from the side of his home with just his fingernail. And all the buildings in Santa Marta were the same. There was no way these walls could stop a bullet. Risking a glance out of the window, Luiz saw the commandos take aim.

'Get down!' he yelled.

He hurled himself on top of Livio as the shack was peppered with gunfire, bullets punching through the walls as though they were made of paper. As slugs ricocheted above him, Luiz curled up into a ball and covered his head with his hands, while Livio yelled in panic.

The barrage seemed to last for an eternity – then, abruptly, there was a booming report from outside, followed by another, and the shooting stopped. Cautiously, Luiz looked up through his fingers. The shack was suddenly very, very still. Shafts of sunlight poured in through the bullet holes in the walls. Crawling on his hands and knees over to the door, Luiz saw that the helicopter had moved off and was circling high in the air above them. The two CORE commandos were lying prostrate on the ground, one clutching his bloodied arm, the other lying stock-still.

In the middle of the square, a tall, dreadlocked figure was calmly reloading his shotgun. Angel gestured wildly up at the helicopter.

'It's me you want!' he roared. 'Come and get me!'

The helicopter circled angrily above the *dono*'s head, its snipers frustrated by the screen of dust and smoke rising up from the square, hiding Angel from their crosshairs. Although the situation looked like a stalemate, in the distance Luiz could hear the rumbling of wheels as CORE's APCs bludgeoned their way through the *favela*. It would be only a matter of minutes before they reached the square.

Luiz turned and looked out through the back door of the shack, which led out to a tiny scrap of land and then a winding alleyway that disappeared off into Santa Marta. Grabbing Livio, he pointed towards it.

'Get out of here!' he shouted.

The MC frowned. 'What?'

'Go fetch your family. Get them out of Santa Marta!'

'Screw that!' Livio shouted back, tapping his gun. 'I'm staying and fighting! I'm Comando Negro!'

'Forget the Comando Negro! They're finished! Even if Trojan can't stop them, then CORE will, or the Compadres, or –'

Luiz stopped, suddenly aware of his slip. Livio's forehead had wrinkled into a frown.

'Trojan?' he repeated, puzzled. 'Who the hell are they?'

As the helicopter thundered overhead, Luiz looked at his friend. He was running out of time to convince him. Maybe the truth was the only way.

'A secret organization. They've come to Rio to take down the Comando Negro.'

'If they're so secret, how come you know about them?'

Luiz took a deep breath. 'I've been working for them.'

A look of incomprehension appeared on Livio's face. 'You're telling me you're a *spy*?'

'No! I mean . . . I can't explain right now. But you've got to believe me – you haven't got a prayer. Running is your only chance!'

'You betrayed us?' the MC muttered to himself disbelievingly.

'I didn't want to, Livio,' Luiz said desperately. 'That's why I came back to warn you. I didn't have any choice!'

'Forget it. I don't want to know.' The MC jabbed a finger

in Luiz's chest. 'I stood up for you. I thought we were friends. I should put a bullet in you, you bastard!'

'I know,' Luiz said simply. 'I'm sorry.'

Livio looked down at his assault rifle, then hurled it angrily to one side. With a final wounded glance, the MC stumbled out of the shack and began running down the alleyway. Luiz felt sick to his stomach. He was about to make his escape after Livio when a cry from the square made him turn back.

The helicopter had returned over the square, strafing bullets over Angel's position. As Angel ducked for cover, there was a flash of orange in the sunlight – a pair of tinted Ray-Bans – and Luiz saw Joker hare across the square to help his brother.

At the same moment, there was a booming crash as an APC erupted into the square from one of the alleyways, its bodywork covered in dents and bits of rubble. Dumbfounded, Joker stopped and stared at the vehicle, completely and utterly exposed. Luiz could only watch helplessly as the APC ground to a halt and the order to fire rang out. A single bullet arrowed unerringly through the air, hitting Joker straight in the neck.

24. Meal Ticket

Luiz watched helplessly as, in slow motion, Joker put a hand to his throat, dropped his gun and collapsed to the ground.

'NO!' howled Angel.

The *dono* broke from his cover and dashed towards his brother, seemingly unconcerned whether or not he was shot too. Grabbing Joker's shirt, Angel dragged his brother's body out from the middle of the square and into the shelter of a side alley. There Angel hugged Joker tightly, then wiped his eyes. Luiz watched with horrified fascination as the *dono* reloaded his shotgun before standing up and gesturing at the commandos.

'You bastards!' he screamed. 'I'll kill you all!'

Angel strode out into the open, firing off round after round from his shotgun at the CORE men sheltering behind their APC. Shocked by the suicidal charge, the commandos shrank back behind the safety of their vehicle. One of them cried out and dropped to the floor, a bullet in his leg; another died instantly from a head wound. Angel walked on, a vengeful devil, even as the return gunfire grew ever more insistent and a blizzard of bullets whizzed around his head.

The dreadful scudding sound had returned: the helicopter had swung around and was making another pass of
the square. Luiz saw Angel stagger as finally one CORE
bullet hit him and then another. He was distracted from
the *dono*'s last moments by the whine of a rocket zeroing
in on him, then the shack exploded and everything went
dark.

Dust. Everywhere there was dust and smoke. Luiz could
taste blood in his mouth. His body was completely
covered in bits of rubble, but he could feel his arms and
legs, and nothing seemed to be broken.

He lay still, hardly daring to breathe. Pricking up his
ears, he realized that the gunfight had stopped in the
square. He heard the helicopter leave – disappearing as
quickly as it had arrived, like a summer storm. After a few
minutes, the APC followed suit, rumbling back down
towards the *boca*. Every so often, there came a defiant
crackle of gunfire, though by the sounds of it the battle
was moving further and further away. With Angel gone,
the Comando Negro would be on the run.

Only when the sky began to darken did Luiz feel safe
enough to push himself free from the rubble and survey
the scene. The square was cloaked in gloom, Joker's body
lying where Angel had left it. Of the *dono*'s corpse, there
was no sign, only the pool of blood where the commandos had shot him.

Santa Marta was like a ghost town. The stereos had
been silenced, the rhythms of the *favela* extinguished.

Shutters had been drawn over the shopfronts and no one was seated at the tables outside the cafes. At the mouth of one alleyway Luiz walked past a woman cradling the body of a child in her arms, blood smeared across its limp limbs. He recognized the boy – one of the *soldados* who guarded the *boca*, he would have felt the full force of CORE's assault.

The mother rocked back and forward in silence, her mouth wide open as though horror had stripped her of her voice. Luiz wanted to stop and help her, but had no idea what he could do or say. How could he make *that* better? Instead he moved on, trying to block out the image of the woman's haunted face from his mind.

Luiz's head was throbbing, his face was cut and his right arm hung limply from his side, but he was alive. Dimly, he wondered whether Livio had managed to escape. The look of betrayal in the MC's eyes as he had fled made Luiz shudder to think about it. Wherever Livio had gone, they would never be friends again. As he trudged down Santa Marta's main street, Luiz realized that there was nothing left for him here any more.

He pulled out his mobile phone and stared at it. Who could he call? Luiz wanted to call his parents, but had no idea where to begin. Trojan? Valerie had told him back in the Mercedes he was on his own. But maybe, with the Comando Negro gone, there was still a chance . . .

Luiz wearily tapped out a number.

'Ricardo's Pizzeria?'

There didn't seem much point in bothering with code

words any more. Instead Luiz said, 'It's Luiz. Tell Jordan it's over.'

It was early in the afternoon the next day and the tables of the Casa Bahia were quiet. The lunchtime crowd had drifted away, leaving only two men sitting in the corner, chatting animatedly with each other over glasses of beer. One was a broad-shouldered *carioca* wearing a leather jacket; the other was a lively British man.

The door opened and a Brazilian teenager walked uncertainly into the restaurant. At the sight of the boy, the British man's face lit up. Rising to his feet, he warmly embraced him.

'Luiz!' Richard Madison exclaimed, slapping him on the back. 'Was I glad to hear that you'd phoned!'

'I guess,' Luiz replied uncertainly.

From the other side of the table, Juan Oliveira leaned over and shook his hand.

'Very impressive work, my friend,' the policeman said. 'You ever think about a job with the police?'

Luiz shook his head. 'I think I've had enough of that kind of thing. I don't want to see another gun as long as I live.'

'Wise words,' Madison said, ushering Luiz into a chair and beckoning to the waitress for another coffee. He continued, in a low undertone, 'It really is a bloody miracle you're alive. When we heard about you and Valerie, and then the CORE raid on Santa Marta, we feared the worst. What happened to the Comando Negro?'

'Most of them died,' Luiz said bluntly. 'The rest fled or got arrested by CORE.'

'So that's it?' asked Madison. 'After all that – there was no mysterious Doctor? It was Angel all along?'

Luiz shrugged. 'Well, it definitely wasn't Cruz. He wanted the Comando Negro out of Santa Marta so he could develop on the land. And if he wasn't the Doctor, then I guess it had to be Angel. Either way, the Comando Negro are finished. Now they're not strong enough to defend the *favela*, another gang will move in for sure. By the end of the week, it'll be the Compadres' cocaine on sale at Santa Marta *boca*. Or Quarto Comando's.'

Mentioning the other gangs made Luiz think of Dog. He wondered whether the little boy would eventually become the new Angel, in charge of Santa Marta. It wouldn't have surprised him. In the Rio *favelas*, there were always new gang members, new *donos* to take the place of those who fell by the wayside.

As the waitress placed a coffee down beside him, Luiz unhooked the gold crucifix from around his neck and tossed it across the table to Madison.

'Guess I won't be needing this any more,' he said. 'I've kept my side of the bargain – now what about Ana?'

Madison grinned. 'Fair's fair. Darius is on the phone as we speak. Your little sister should be out of jail by the end of the day.' Glancing at Luiz, his smile faded. 'I thought you might be a bit happier to hear that news.'

'No, I am happy . . . it's just . . .' Luiz searched for the right words, but failed. 'It's been a tough time, you know?' he said finally.

'Yes, of course.' Madison nodded. 'Listen, it's going to take Darius a bit of time to do his thing. Why don't we have some food while we're here? I've heard the menu's uncommonly good and I'm starving.'

'Music to my ears,' a voice said smoothly behind them.

Luiz looked up to see a small man standing over their table, impeccably dressed in a crisp blue shirt and suit trousers, his face graced by an elegantly trimmed beard. Luiz recognized him from the stake-out of the Casa Bahia – it was Ivan Fernandes, owner of the restaurant.

Fernandes gave Oliveira a polite nod. 'Good afternoon, sir. I'm delighted to have such a valued customer visiting us again.'

'I bet you are, Ivan,' the policeman replied drily. 'The amount of money I spend here, I should be a partner. How's the crab today?'

'We had a fresh delivery this morning,' replied Fernandes with a smile. 'Sadly, I have a pressing engagement at home, but rest assured that Marissa here will take good care of you.'

As the pretty waitress smiled shyly and took out her pad, Fernandes bowed and left the table. Luiz stood up.

'I'm going to the toilet,' he said.

'Are you not going to order anything?' Oliveira asked. 'The food really is good here, you know?'

'Maybe later,' Luiz said. 'I'm not hungry right now.'

Moving away from the table, he disappeared down the dark passageway that led to the toilets. After the fighting and the bloody deaths he had witnessed, the last thing Luiz wanted to do was eat. All he wanted was to get Ana back and go home.

Beyond the main restaurant, the Casa Bahia was a warren of corridors and passageways. Finally locating the toilets, Luiz splashed water on his face and wearily rubbed his eyes. On his way back to the table, he got completely lost, pushing through a door only to find himself standing outside, in a loading bay behind the building. A pile of empty crates had been stacked up outside the back door, having been unloaded of their cargo: ingredients, Luiz supposed, maybe the fresh crab Fernandes had mentioned a moment ago in the restaurant.

As his eyes flicked over the crates, Luiz noticed that a giant crack was running along the side of one of them. He ran a finger down the crack, astonished. It looked exactly like the crate Livio had dropped the day before – only then it had been filled with packages of cocaine. It seemed impossible, but it had to be the same one. When CORE had attacked Santa Marta, Angel had ordered that the crates be taken back to the holding warehouse downtown. So what in God's name was one now doing outside the Casa Bahia?

As Luiz stared at the crates, Jordan's words about the Doctor ran through his mind: *Maybe he's a legitimate businessman, someone with a good reason to have trucks going back and forth across the border.* A chill ran down Luiz's spine. They had all been wrong. There was a Doctor, and he had met Angel at Casa Bahia, but it wasn't Jorge Cruz. It was Ivan Fernandes.

If Luiz was right, the man they had been looking for had just walked out the front of the restaurant. He was about to rush back inside and tell Madison and Oliveira when something else caught his eye, a distinctive red mark on the floor in front of him. Blood. Frowning, Luiz touched the bloodstain. It was still warm. Whoever had bled here, they had done it recently.

Luiz turned round and found himself standing face to face with Angel.

25. Gatecrashers

'You lying piece of shit,' Angel said through clenched teeth. 'Stripe was right. You are a grass.'

He hadn't died after all. Somehow the *dono* had managed to escape from the CORE forces, but the man standing in front of Luiz wasn't the calm, forceful gang leader Luiz had come to know. Angel was huddled up against the back wall of the restaurant, his long trench coat buttoned up in spite of the heat. Sweat glistened on his forehead and his face was streaked with tears. Angel's pupils were unnaturally large and his movements had an edgy quality to them that suggested he had been taking a lot of drugs. He was still carrying his 12-gauge shotgun, which was aimed directly at Luiz.

Slowly, Luiz held up his hands.

'I'm no grass, I swear!'

Without warning Angel lunged forward and smashed the butt of his gun into Luiz's stomach. Luiz crumpled to the floor, bent double in agony.

'Don't lie to me,' the *dono* hissed. 'I saw you inside with your friends. You think I can't tell what kind of guys they are? They're cops! You've been playing us for fools all along – and we treated you like a *brother*!'

The *dono* reached down, grabbed Luiz by the hair and smacked his head on the ground. Luiz heard a sickening crack and felt shooting pains race across his skull.

'I had no choice, Angel!' Luiz cried out. 'My sister . . . they were going to put her in prison!'

'A sister? Really? I used to have a brother, Luiz – remember him? Remember Joker? Remember when he got shot in the throat?' Angel's voice cracked with hysteria.

'That wasn't anything to do with me, I'm telling you! I ran to Santa Marta to try and warn you!'

'Too little, too late,' Angel said ominously.

'Please let me go,' Luiz begged, looking up at the *dono* through watering eyes. 'I won't say anything, I promise. Everyone thinks you're dead. You can get away – no one will know!'

'Where do I go, Luiz? Santa Marta's all I know. I've got nothing there now. Where exactly should I go, wise guy?'

'I don't know,' Luiz said desperately. 'Get out of Rio – start over somewhere new.'

Angel placed his foot on Luiz's chest and pressed his weight down upon him, nestling the barrel of his shotgun up against the boy's throat.

'Here's a better idea,' he said conversationally. 'I'm going to go to Ivan Fernandes's house. I'm going to see him. Then I'm going to kill him.'

'Kill the Doctor?' gasped Luiz. 'Why?'

'Because he betrayed me, just like you did. The Doctor promised that he would protect us, that he could pay the police off so they'd leave us alone. Now Rafael's dead and the Doctor's still got all his money and his business and his life. So I'm going to even up the score. And you're going to help me.'

'Me? What can I do? I'm begging you, leave me out of this.'

'No, no, no!' Angel shouted emphatically, pressing his foot down harder on Luiz's chest. 'You are Comando Negro, Luiz! No one leaves the Comando Negro. I'm ordering you to drive me to the Doctor's place now or, God help me, Luiz, I'll shoot you in the head right now. Do you understand me?'

Luiz understood, all right. He nodded quickly. After a wary pause, Angel lifted up his foot, allowing Luiz to pick himself gingerly up off the ground.

'My truck's around the corner,' Angel said. 'We'll take that.'

The *dono* prodded Luiz in the back with his shotgun, forcing him to move. As he walked away from the restaurant, Luiz remembered with a jolt that he had just given back his GPS crucifix. Without it, there was no way he could contact Madison or anyone else at Trojan. He was on his own.

Over the course of the past week Luiz had witnessed enough violence and brutality to last him a lifetime. He had seen people shot in front of his eyes and had nearly lost his own life on more than one occasion. But even after all that there was a nightmarish quality to his journey with Angel that somehow surpassed anything else he had seen.

The death of his brother had broken the *dono*, reducing a proud man to tatters. His eyes wild, he chopped up long lines of cocaine on the dashboard, unsteadily snorting them through a banknote as the truck bounced about on the uneven road surface. He was so high that he didn't seem to care whether the police saw him, not even bothering to wipe the residue of white powder from his nose.

However, without the drugs, it was doubtful whether Angel would have still been on his feet. Even though he had survived the shoot-out with CORE, it had taken a heavy toll. At one point he winced suddenly, doubling up in pain. Looking over, Luiz saw a trickle of blood collecting at Angel's feet.

'Jesus!' he cried. 'You're still bleeding! We have to go to the hospital!'

'Shut up and keep driving,' growled Angel. 'It's not that much further now.'

The *dono* directed him west, along the southern coastal road out of Rio. They were heading for Barra da Tijuca, a suburb that boasted some of the city's most expensive properties. Here foreign businessmen and wealthy *cariocas* maintained luxurious houses set back from the picturesque shoreline in secure gated communities.

As Luiz drove on through the bright afternoon sunshine, Angel slumped back in his seat, staring dully at the road ahead. He seemed to be slipping in and out of consciousness. If it hadn't been for the shotgun lying menacingly in the *dono*'s lap, Luiz would have been tempted to pull over, or try and slip his mobile phone out of his pocket to call

Richard Madison. But with Angel so unstable, it would have been suicide to try anything. All Luiz could do was pray that Madison and Oliveira had realized something had gone wrong. But even if they had, he wasn't sure what they could do about it.

Things were looking bleak. If the worst happened and he died, would Trojan tell his family how and why? He very much doubted it. Would Luiz's foster parents and Ana spend the rest of their lives not knowing whether he was alive or not? Would they think that he had just walked out on them?

'Pull over here,' Angel muttered.

Luiz stopped the truck at the side of the road. To his left, a paved driveway ran up towards a set of high metal railings. Through the gaps in the bars, he could see a palatial stucco house painted gleaming white. Two men in security outfits were standing guard either side of the gates.

'What are we going to do now?' Luiz asked. 'How do we get past the gates?'

Angel made an impatient sound.

'We're in a truck, aren't we? Put your foot down and drive through them!'

'What? Even if we make it through the gates, those guys are armed, Angel!'

'It's up to you,' Angel replied coldly, levelling his shotgun. 'You can die over there or die right here.'

'Listen,' Luiz tried desperately. 'We know that Fernandes is the Doctor. Let me call the police. I know people who can keep you out of jail. It'll be all right, I promise.'

'Drive!' Angel bellowed.

Gritting his teeth, Luiz jammed his foot down on the accelerator. As the truck suddenly lurched towards the gates, the security guards waved frantically for it to slow down, fumbling for their weapons. Before they could fire a shot, the truck bounced in between them and crashed headlong into the gates.

The gates buckled and flew open, the impact sending Luiz flying painfully into his steering wheel. As he cried out, the truck veered wildly to the left, crashing into a low wall that ran alongside the driveway. Before the wheels had stopped spinning, Angel had climbed out of the truck and begun firing at the guards. As one of them fell, the other began sprinting down the main road. Angel turned away, instantly dismissing him.

The echo of the last gunshot faded away, leaving the estate in a state of eerie quiet.

Angel strode round to the driver's seat and dragged Luiz out of the car. 'Come on – we're not done yet.' Reaching into his waistband, the *dono* tossed Luiz a pistol. 'Here. You'll need this.'

Luiz stared dumbly at the gun. 'You're giving me a weapon?'

'No going back now.' Angel shrugged. 'Fernandes's guards will shoot you just as quickly as they will me. We're both dead men. Only hope now is to take the Doctor down with us.'

Still limping and holding his belly, Angel dragged himself up the driveway towards the mansion. It was as though he had already forgotten about Luiz. Frantically, Luiz pulled out his mobile phone and dialled Trojan's number. This time the call went straight through to Richard Madison.

'Luiz! What's happened? Where are you?'

'At Ivan Fernandes's house. He's the Doctor! And now Angel's going to –'

There was a loud pinging sound and a plant pot beside Luiz exploded. Whirling round, Luiz saw two men running towards him from the side of the mansion, assault rifles raised.

Madison was shouting something down the mobile phone, but Luiz couldn't hear what he was saying. As another storm of bullets came towards him, he dived over the wall and into the flower bed on the other side, the phone slipping from his grasp. Luiz flattened himself into the dirt, flinching every time a bullet bit into the wall.

Given that Angel had already disappeared inside Fernandes's house, Luiz knew there was no way he could last out here on his own. His only hope was to hare across the lawn towards the front door of the mansion, which had been left invitingly ajar. He could cover the open ground in maybe five, ten seconds. But with the guards fast approaching, he would be shot dead after three.

He needed cover. Poking his head up from behind the wall, Luiz fired off a couple of shots in the general direction of the guards. He heard shouts of alarm and the gunfire abruptly ceased.

It was now or never. Taking a deep breath, Luiz jumped to his feet and ran for his life.

26. Face-Off

As fast as he ran, time seemed to slow down for Luiz. Each second lasted an eternity. The slightest detail took on significance: from the feel of the springy lawn beneath his feet to the sing-song choruses of the birds high up in the trees. One step, then another. Luiz's heart was raggedly thudding in his chest. The doorway to Fernandes's house loomed up in front of him, a dark portal to safety.

The first gunshot went off sooner than he had been expecting, zinging over his shoulder and spurring him onwards. The two guards had reached the corner of the house and were racing towards him along the driveway. As Luiz hurdled over a flower bed and raced up the steps on to the veranda, there was another blast and a chunk of wood flew off one of the white balustrade posts. He threw himself headlong towards the door, landing inside the house even as the veranda was enveloped in a hail of bullets behind him.

It was gloomy inside, shadows stretching out across the spotless tiled floor. There was no sign of either Angel or the Doctor. Scrambling to his feet, Luiz ran down the hallway and through a door that led into a brightly lit kitchen.

The room was silent, save for the soft humming of the fridge. Luiz stood stock-still, holding his breath.

The front door creaked open again as the guards followed him into the house, their soft footfalls audible as they crept inside. Luiz looked down at his gun. Even now, with his life in the balance, he wasn't sure that he could shoot someone. He glanced around the kitchen, but saw nothing among the household appliances on the sideboard that could help him. Pressing himself against the wall by the door, he waited as the footsteps drew nearer.

The kitchen door opened a crack and the barrel of an assault rifle poked cautiously into the room. Luiz waited until the man was halfway through the doorway, then he kicked the door as hard as he could. There was a loud oath as the gun fell to the floor, which turned into a growl of rage as Luiz kicked the rifle out of reach. The guard burst into the kitchen, throwing a clumsy haymaker at Luiz, who ducked sharply. Luiz then responded with a deft punch to the man's kidneys, followed up by a knee into his groin. As the guard buckled, Luiz brought his pistol down sharply on the man's head. The guard grunted and went sprawling headlong across the tiles, unconscious.

'Hold it right there,' said a clipped voice.

Luiz looked up to see that the second guard had appeared in the kitchen. Before he could react, a booming shot rang out. As the guard fell to the floor, dead, Angel appeared in the doorway behind him, his shotgun still smoking.

'Angel!' Luiz gasped. 'You saved me!'

'I know,' the *dono* replied flatly. 'I guess we're in this together now.'

A reflective look flickered across Angel's face and for a brief second he seemed a lot younger than he had before. Then, his resolve hardening, he turned on his heel and marched back into the hallway. Glancing around at the expensive paintings and ornaments with undisguised hatred, he smashed a slender vase with the butt of his shotgun.

'Where are you hiding, Fernandes?' he cried out. 'Come out and face me, you son of a bitch!'

'Maybe he heard us coming and ran away,' Luiz suggested.

The *dono* shook his head. 'He's here, all right. I can smell him.' He jerked his head in the direction of the staircase. 'I'm going upstairs. You stay down here and look for him.'

With that, Angel marched upstairs and disappeared inside one of the bedrooms. Luiz glanced at the front door. He could make a run for it, take a chance that there were no guards waiting for him outside, but what if the Doctor was still in the house somewhere? After everything, he couldn't bear the thought that Fernandes might escape. Angel was right: they were in it together now.

Stealing across the ground floor of the house, Luiz found himself in a large room dominated by a long dining table. Sunlight poured in through a window that ran the length of the room, glinting off a mirror hanging on the far wall. Through the window, a sandy beach was visible, with surf pounding down relentlessly upon it. Luiz looked out over the view.

'Are you lost, boy?'

Luiz whirled round and saw Ivan Fernandes staring back at him. The restaurateur was standing on the other side of the table from him, his back to the mirror. The smooth, polite facade he had displayed in the Casa Bahia had vanished, replaced by a disdainful sneer. In his hand Fernandes brandished a pearl-handled Colt .45 pistol, its barrel pointing straight at Luiz's head.

'Don't move,' he said matter-of-factly. 'You were at the restaurant. With the policeman.'

Luiz nodded dumbly.

'And now you're here. In my house. With a gun.'

'I know who you are!' Luiz shouted bravely. 'You're the Doctor!'

Fernandes raised a cold eyebrow. 'Really? Come here to arrest me, have you?'

'And I've phoned the police,' Luiz lied. 'They're on their way, and if anything happens to me they'll think it was you.'

'The police will think what I tell them,' Fernandes countered. 'To them, you're just another petty thief from the slums who's about to be shot dead by a respectable man guarding his property. You need to be bit quicker if you're going to try and outwit me.'

A dark shadow flitted across the mirror behind Fernandes and suddenly Angel was in the room with them.

'This quick enough?' the *dono* whispered, pressing his

shotgun against the side of the Doctor's head. 'Drop it. Now.'

Fernandes froze, shock etched upon his face. Luiz could see his mind racing, calculating whether there was any way he could fight back. Then his shoulders slumped and he dropped the Colt to the floor with a clatter.

'What the hell are you doing, Angel?' he grimaced. 'Have you gone crazy?'

'I'm the sanest I've been in a long time,' Angel replied. 'I was crazy when I listened to you. I was crazy when I believed that you could protect us from the police.'

He jabbed the Doctor's head with his gun. In a flash Fernandes's cool demeanour had been stripped away and, when he spoke again, fear trembled at the edge of his voice.

'I did everything I could!' he protested. 'I spent a fortune bribing officials to cover your rotten backs – policemen, politicians. But once that Jorge Cruz got involved, we were finished!'

'No, the Comando Negro were finished. Seems to me you're still doing pretty well for yourself, Fernandes.'

'Think of all I've done for you, Angel!' Fernandes tried desperately. 'When I first hired you, you were a nothing in the Compadres. Now you're the most feared gangster in Rio!'

'Maybe so,' Angel said. 'But at least when I was a nothing I had a brother. Some things aren't worth the price you pay for them.'

Keeping the Doctor at arm's length, Angel pushed him

into the centre of the room with the barrel of his Remington. Fernandes closed his eyes, as though he had resigned himself to his fate.

'This is for Rafael,' Angel said, through clenched teeth. His finger tightened on the trigger.

'Wait!' Luiz cried out.

Taking a deep breath, he stepped forward and pointed his gun at Angel, trying to ignore the fact that his hands were trembling.

'Don't shoot him.'

'Luiz?' A look of astonishment crossed the *dono*'s face. 'What the hell are you doing?'

'Getting involved. Put your gun down.'

'Or what?' Angel retorted, a challenge in his voice. 'You'll shoot me?'

'I don't want to. Part of me wants you to kill Fernandes. But I've seen enough dead bodies as it is and I don't want to see another one. Fernandes should go to jail, where he belongs.'

'Who cares about jail?' the *dono* yelled. 'Rafael's dead!'

'Let this one go, Angel. Please.'

Distracted, Angel momentarily lowered his shotgun. Fernandes broke free and pulled something from his pocket. Metal gleamed in the sunlight. A blade. Fernandes spun round and drove the dagger deep into Angel's chest. The *dono* staggered backwards, crashing into the mirror, his hands clutching feebly at the hilt of the dagger. Angel's eyes rolled up in his head and he slumped to the ground.

Luiz's eyes met the Doctor's. Then, dropping to one

knee, he took aim and fired. The bullet clipped Ivan Fernandes in the right shoulder and the man fell to the floor, screaming in agony.

Luiz stayed kneeling down, all of a sudden feeling strangely detached. His arms tingled from the recoil of the weapon and the smell of cordite hung heavy in the air. Slowly straightening up, he walked across the room and levelled the gun at the Doctor.

'Make one move,' Luiz said softly, 'and I'll kill you. I swear.'

Fernandes was clutching his shoulder, making high-pitched whimpering sounds. It was just the two of them now. Luiz could put a bullet in his skull and no one would ever know about it. This drug-dealing murderer would be gone. He brought up his left hand and took aim.

'Luiz?'

Luiz started. Glancing up, he saw Juan Oliveira standing in the doorway. The policeman looked out of breath.

'Juan?' said Luiz, his voice trembling. 'How did you get here?'

'Traced your mobile phone call. I'm here now. It's OK.'

'It's not OK!' Luiz shot back. 'Can't you see?' He pointed at Angel. 'He's dead and it's my fault. Everyone's dead – apart from Fernandes. He can't get away with it!'

'He won't get away with it,' Oliveira said. 'He'll go to prison. I promise. You need to put the gun down, Luiz.'

The policeman walked slowly towards him, maintaining eye contact all the while. Folding his hands over Luiz's gun, he gently removed it from his grasp. As they stared at one another, Fernandes began sobbing with relief at their feet.

Luiz felt a wave of nausea wash over him. Dimly, he was aware that Oliveira had put an arm around his shoulders.

'It's all right, son. Come on.'

A wailing police siren had struck up in the distance. In a daze, Luiz trudged out of the house and into the bright sunshine, leaving Oliveira standing over the shaking figure of the Doctor and the bloodied corpse of the leader of the Comando Negro.

27. Endgame

Early the next morning, a cable car climbed up through the air above Rio, heading towards the summit of Sugarloaf Mountain. On a bright, clear day the whole of Rio would have been visible through the windows, but now the city was smothered beneath a thick blanket of early-morning mist. Rain drummed impatiently on the cable car roof.

Given the weather, it was little surprise that the cable car was quiet, most of the tourists preferring to wait for the mist to clear. Only a group of Germans had braved the journey in the hope of a sudden burst of sunshine. They stood at the far end of the car, keeping a wary distance from the only other occupant: a teenage boy staring out into the whiteness, his face covered in cuts and bruises. To the Germans – who had been warned about the young gang members from the *favelas* – he looked like trouble.

Lost in his own thoughts, Luiz was barely aware that anyone was looking at him. The turmoil of the previous few days was starting to catch up with him. He was aware that he was on the verge of crashing with exhaustion. Not yet, though. There was still one more thing he had to do.

He had spent the night at Juan Oliveira's, the policeman patching up his wounds as best he could. They sat in front of the TV, watching news reports showing the aftermath of the carnage at Fernandes's house. The reporter hailed the arrest of the Doctor as a triumph for the intelligence services and the police. There was no mention of Trojan Industries or Luiz. The camera suddenly cut to an interview with Jorge Cruz, who beamed with delight as he praised the efforts of the police. Luiz snorted dismissively and changed the channel.

Later that evening, Trojan Industries called Oliveira to pass on the word that Ana had been released and told Luiz to meet them on top of Sugarloaf Mountain at nine o'clock the next morning. Why on earth they had decided to meet in such an out-of-the-way place, Luiz couldn't begin to understand. Oliveira had offered to come with him, but the next morning a call from his bosses had sent him hurrying to the station instead. They said goodbye quickly, respect on both sides. No matter what Luiz thought about some of the cops who worked in Rio, Oliveira was a good man.

Now, as the cable car continued to scale up the mountain, rocking slightly in the breeze, Luiz was acutely aware that he was meeting Trojan alone. For reasons he couldn't entirely put his finger on, that made him apprehensive. Ahead of him the dark silhouette of the cable-car station loomed out of the mist. The trajectory of their ascent flattened and then they came to a juddering standstill at the top of the mountain.

As the doors opened, Luiz zipped up his jacket and stepped out into the fresh air. Though the drizzle had abated, the view was still obscured by a swirling white mass. From memory Luiz knew that the summit of Sugarloaf was little more than a rocky outcrop. There was nothing up here save for a lone drinks stand, which rewarded the more adventurous types who had ascended on foot.

Looking around him, Luiz caught sight of a tall figure standing by the guardrail, peering out hopefully into the mist. It was Darius Jordan. The head of Trojan was dressed in a long grey overcoat and carried a briefcase in one hand. Just like a normal businessman. Seeing Jordan calmly standing there, Luiz couldn't help but feel resentment wash over him for everything that he had been forced to go through.

At the sound of Luiz's footsteps, the American turned round and smiled. 'Luiz! You got here all right?'

'I guess,' muttered Luiz. 'Could we not have done this downtown?'

'Perhaps you're right,' Jordan agreed. 'Believe it or not, I've spent the best part of two weeks stuck inside that warehouse and I just wanted to see Rio before I left.' He gestured wryly at the fog. 'I thought it was going to be a nice day.'

Behind them, the Germans had bustled over to the opposite side of the summit, leaving Luiz and Jordan entirely alone.

'It might still be a nice day,' said Luiz warily. 'But it's pretty lonely up here right now.'

Jordan frowned. 'What do you mean? Why do you think I told you to meet me here?'

As Luiz shifted his stance, muscles tensing in case he had to run or fight, realization dawned on Jordan's face. 'Do you think I asked you here so I could *kill* you?'

'Maybe,' Luiz replied defensively. 'After all, you don't need me any more. Maybe you want to make sure I don't talk to anybody.'

The American barked with laughter. 'Jesus, Luiz, you don't think much of us, do you? We're not callous murderers – we're good guys trying to stop some very bad people. I'd love it if we could play by the rules, but it doesn't work like that. The world's not black and white. After all you've seen, surely you can understand that?'

Luiz shrugged.

'Don't you know how grateful we are?' Jordan asked. 'Thanks to you, Trojan's first mission has been classed as a success. We're free to continue our operations. We're flying out of Rio this morning.'

'Oh? Where are you going?'

'I don't know yet. Could be anywhere. The Comando Negro isn't the only gang in the world. This is a global problem, my friend.'

'So you're going to go to another country and you'll make someone else do what I did?' There was a challenge in Luiz's voice.

Jordan sighed. 'We didn't *make* you do anything. We didn't put Ana in jail. You could have walked out of my office, phoned your parents and taken it from there. I told you at the time, Luiz – there's always a choice. Maybe, in a while, you'll see that.' The American held out his hand. 'Shall we shake hands before we go?'

Luiz thought back over everything that had happened to him in the past fortnight: his sister's arrest, the fights with the Compadres and Quarto Comando, Joker's death, Angel's death, the look in Livio's eyes when he realized that he had been betrayed . . .

'Go screw yourself,' said Luiz.

Jordan nodded slowly and withdrew his hand. 'I had hoped you might see it differently. A lot of good things came out of this. A violent gang has been broken up, a massive drug-smuggling network has been exposed. The Doctor will spend the rest of his life in prison. And, perhaps most importantly . . .'

He turned and pointed over to the drinks stand. Through the gloom, Luiz could see three figures: two adults and a smaller figure. He recognized the two adults – Richard Madison, who gave him a cheery wave, and Valerie Singer, who took an expressionless drag on her cigarette, and between them –

'Luiz!' cried Ana Alves.

His sister came tearing towards him and threw her arms around him, sobbing violently. Ana's clothes were bedraggled and grimy, and she was shaking, but she was alive. Luiz hugged her numbly, barely able to believe that she was actually standing there with him.

'Are you OK?' he said. 'You're not hurt?'

'No, I'm fine. Just happy to be out of jail. I never want to go back there again.'

As he hugged his sister, he saw Darius Jordan smile at him. After a pause, Luiz gave him a nod of recognition. Maybe it had been worth it, after all.

Ana looked up at him, her face streaked with tears. 'I'm so sorry, Luiz. I promise I'll never do anything like that again.'

'It's OK,' Luiz said quietly. 'You're safe now. That's all that matters.'

'I couldn't believe when those people came to get me out,' Ana continued. 'They've been really kind.'

Glancing up, Luiz saw that Darius Jordan was no longer standing beside them, and Richard Madison and Valerie Singer had disappeared from the front of the drinks stand. The only people visible on Sugarloaf's summit were the German tourists, who talked excitedly among themselves as the first ray of sunshine cut through the mist. Trojan had vanished.

'Where have they gone?' Ana asked quietly.

'I don't know,' Luiz replied truthfully. 'But I don't think we're going to see them again.'

'They didn't even tell me their names.'

'Yeah, they're like that. You've got more important things to worry about anyway. By my reckoning, we've only got a few hours to get back home before Mum and Dad arrive.' Luiz grinned. 'And you might want to have a shower before then. Did they not have soap in jail?'

Ana punched him playfully on the arm. 'Speak for yourself, sweaty! You smell like a goat! And what happened to your face? Have you been fighting again?'

'It's a long story. Maybe I'll tell you on the way down. Can we get off this mountain now?'

Ana looked out wistfully over the guardrail at the brightening sky.

'Look,' she said, 'the sun's starting to come out. Now that we're here, can we not wait for a few minutes – just until the mist clears?'

Luiz sighed. 'I guess so.'

Brother and sister stood side by side, watching in silence as the fog burned away and the sun came out over their city.

EPILOGUE: Home Time

Luiz stood quietly outside the front of his house, leaning against the bumper of the mud-stained Jeep now parked in the driveway. His foster parents had returned home an hour ago, laden down with suitcases and presents. As he hugged his mum and dad, Luiz was suddenly overwhelmed by the realization that it was over. His shoulders slumped and he had to fight back the tears springing into his eyes. He had survived.

The family sat down together in the lounge, drinking coffee as Mariella and Francesco told them all about their trip to São Paulo. It seemed they had stumbled across a major story while they were away which would be the headline story in *O Globo* the next morning. When it came to their children's turn, Luiz and Ana tried not to look each other in the eye as they glibly answered questions about school and the past couple of weeks. Luiz explained away his injuries by saying that he had fallen off the back of a scooter. His mum had given him a suspicious look, but appeared to accept it. Luiz didn't like lying to his foster parents, but he couldn't think of a way to tell them the truth. Where would he begin?

Faced with a barrage of normality, it was a relief to escape outside, breathe in the cool evening air and listen to the chirping of birds perched in the trees.

There was a noise in the driveway behind Luiz and Ana appeared at his side, slipping her arm through his and resting her head on his shoulder. Refreshed by a shower and a change of clothes, the colour was already returning to his sister's cheeks.

'I can't quite believe it,' she said thoughtfully. 'Are we really going to get away with it? Mum and Dad aren't going to find out?'

'Looks like it.' Luiz shot her a sideways glance. 'Long as you can keep your big mouth shut.'

Ana giggled. 'I think you can trust me on that one. I still don't know how you did it – how you got me out of jail. You're not going to tell me, are you?'

Luiz shook his head. 'No. Maybe one day.'

'Are you sure? I get the feeling it could make a really good story for the newspaper . . .'

'You've got to be kidding me!'

Ana laughed. 'Maybe a little bit. I think I'm going to take a break from journalism – just for a while, though.'

'Don't leave it too long,' Luiz murmured, his eyes straying back up towards Santa Marta. 'There's a big story involving Councillor Cruz that people need to read about and I've got the scoop on it. I'll tell you about that, if you want.'

Ana paused, following Luiz's gaze up towards the hillside *favela*. 'You still want to go back there, don't you? To Santa Marta?'

Which was a question he had been asking himself. Luiz thought about it for a moment.

'No,' he said finally. 'There's nothing there for me any more.'

Ana's eyes went suddenly serious. 'Are you OK?'

Luiz took a last look at Santa Marta, then smiled at his sister.

'Yeah, I'm fine. Let's go inside.'

'If I were you, I'd stay out here,' Ana said mischievously. 'Mum's sure you've been fighting again, and she's not happy.'

Luiz chuckled softly. 'I've handled worse. Come on.'

As he led his sister back inside their house, the sun dipping behind Rio's hillsides, a blast of automatic fire echoed down from the *favela* through the encroaching darkness. Business as usual.

DON'T MISS THE NEXT
HEART-STOPPING
ADVENTURE

GANG
LANDS
RUSSIA

NEW COUNTRY.
NEW GANG.
All-NEW ACTION.

COMING MAY 2010

6 BOOKS THAT MATTER

6 books we fell in love with – and you will too.
As chosen by the Spinebreakers crew

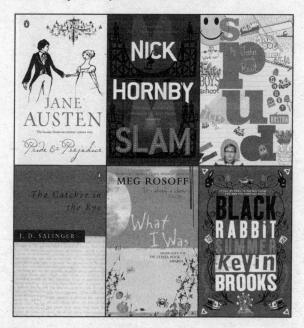

The list continues at spinebreakers.co.uk

DO YOU WANT TO JOIN THE CREW?

If you are a story-surfer, word-lover, day-dreamer,
reader/writer/artist/thinker . . . BECOME one of us

spinebreakers

spinebreakers.co.uk

GET INSIDE YOUR FAVOURITE BOOK